IGNORANCE
IS BLISS

MATTHEW LEDREW

IGNORANCE IS BLISS

CORAL BEACH CASEFILES

Published in Canada by Engen Books, St. John's, NL.

Library and Archives Canada Cataloguing in Publication
LeDrew, Matthew, 1984-
    Ignorance is bliss / Matthew LeDrew.
(Black womb ; 6)
ISBN 978-1-926903-01-9
    I. Title. II. Series: LeDrew, Matthew, 1984- .
Black womb ; 6.
PS8623.E424I56 2010   C813'.6   C2010-905481-4

Second Edition ISBN: 978-1-989473-08-5

Distributed by:
Engen Books
www.engenbooks.com
submissions@engenbooks.com

First mass market paperback printing: October 2010
Second mass market paperback printing: July 2019

Cover Image: Kit Sora Photography

For
Ellen

CHAPTER ONE:
YOUTH

"Is that what you're wearing to the dance?" Julie Peterson snapped sardonically. She peered up from her vanity long enough to glare at the younger girl, giving her a once over. She turned back toward the mirror and finished applying her scarlet lipstick, smacked her lips together once, then pressed them against a napkin to remove the excess.

The younger girl, Mandy Peterson, spread her arms and looked down at herself, then stretched to look at her own backside. She was wearing a dark blue sweater she'd picked up at the Gap, which wasn't hard to tell, as there were big bold letters across the front that read 'GAP.' Her jeans were baggy and loose, and needed the aid of a rather large belt with a buckle in the shape of Texas to help hold them up. "What's wrong with this?"

Julie rolled her eyes, bunched up the napkin and then tossed it into a nearby trash can. It was blue with hearts printed all over it. She was wearing a loose, red sleeveless shirt with a high slit in one side that came up to meet her underarms.

An older generation would have said that it looked like rags on her. Only Julie could make rags look so good.

With it she wore tight black pants with silver leopard spots that she'd painted on herself. They shimmered in the right light. They hung low on her hips, so much so that her pink lace thong was showing.

"There's nothing wrong with it." she admitted with a sigh, smiling over her shoulder at her cousin. "I just think that you're overdoing the whole beggar theme, is all."

Mandy turned away and crossed her arms. "I think you're overdoing the whole 'slut without a cause' theme."

"What?" Julie snapped, turning just in time to see the girl walk out her bedroom door.

"Nothing." Mandy waved as she disappeared into her room to change again.

Julie frowned, then turned back to her mirror.

ʎ⟨⟩ʎ

Mandy shuffled through the boxes of clothes in her closet, sifting through them to try and find anything she could wear. She held up an elegant red dress, mulled over it for a minute, then shoved it back into the box and moved on.

"What are you getting so dressed up for, anyway?" she called out across the hall, poking her head out of her closet just long enough to make sure Julie was still there. She was, carefully applying mascara to her lashes. "Is Xander going to be there?"

Julie smiled with one side of her face, her lips curling at the end like a 40s villain's mustache. "He'd better be.

And I swear, if he wears that ratty old Transformers tee-shirt again, I'll wring his puny neck."

Mandy was holding a large turquoise gown with puffy frills across the chest.

"Not that one, hun. The blue, maybe?" Julie suggested, trying to find a nice way of disapproving her relative's taste in clothing lately.

"So, are you two, like, dating now, or something?" Mandy asked, trying to make the question sound uninvolved and casual as she searched to find the shirt Julie was talking about.

"Or something." Julie huffed with a laugh, putting her makeup away and walking across the hall to Mandy's room. She poked her head into the closet. "Not that blue one. Don't wanna show that much skin."

"What I was thinking," Mandy agreed, giving the blue tank top a curt nod of disapproval before shoving it into the dark reaches of her closet. "What were you saying about Xander?"

"Alex," Julie corrected, giving Mandy a tap on the head. "His name is Alex."

Mandy turned quizzically. "He doesn't like being called Xander?"

"No... I don't. It sounds stupid. Nobody's name begins with an X."

"Xander's does," Mandy pointed out cheerily.

Julie growled, then picked up a Cherry Coke that had been resting atop Mandy's dresser and took a sip through the slender dual straws. Tilting her head to make her brunette hair fall away from her face, she reminded herself to do something else with it.

Mandy made the same motion with her own auburn hair but chose to leave it the way it was. She eyed the foundation and lipstick on her dresser, pouting out one of her thin, delicate lips so that she could see it if she strained.

"Scarlet does the trick really well." Julie laughed as she handed Mandy the Coke. "Or Strawberry Rouge, but stay away from pink and anything resembling flesh tones... they'll make your lips disappear completely."

Mandy smiled.

Julie walked over to the dresser, selected the strawberry, then tossed it over to her. "And there's nothing going on with me and Xander Drew."

"Bull!" Mandy giggled, taking the top off of the lipstick and applying it without the aid of a mirror. "I saw you two looking all chummy in school the other day. He couldn't keep his eyes off you."

Julie said nothing, then slowly turned, smiling. "He was into me, wasn't he?"

"Like a magnet!" the younger girl agreed. "I don't know how he can keep his hands off you!"

"Oh, believe me, he manages," Julie frowned. "But, it's nothing big... yet. We're still at the 'friends with benefits' stage right now, and I've got no clue how to get it forward. Everything I've ever learned about men I have to forget when I'm around Alex. He plays by a whole different set of rules."

Mandy paused, nodding silently as she took that in. Finally, she smiled. "What kind of benefits?"

Julie laughed, picking up a shirt and tossing it at her.

That's Julie, all over and covered in whipped cream, thought Mandy as she scribbled into her notebook with a pink feathered pen. She dotted all her I's with carefully crafted little happy faces, then coloured them in with the yellow highlighter that lay on the bed at her side. She sighed every time she did so, as if it were necessary to the process. *She tries so hard to be, like, deep or something. To not kiss and tell and to not drag the boys into the dark closets, but it doesn't take much pushing to get her to break. It's not her fault. It's not even a bad thing, really. It's just who she is.*

Her relationship with Xander... sorry, Alexander, *is, at best, terminal. To-be-historic. Dead in the water. He's a Leo and she's a Capricorn. Seriously, need I say more? Well, he's all stoic and broody. He likes to curl up in his bat-cave and grumble a lot and stuff like that. She's more open. She wants to be out in the daylight where everyone can see her... probably doing something that should not be seen by anyone else. They're so, like, wrong for each other, that it's a miracle they never got together before. 'Cause you know that's the way it always happens. We all end up with the totally wrong person for us.*

Just look at Mike Harris and Cathy Kennessy.

॓Υ॓

"I think yesterday's storm fried a few transistors in here," Mike offered, taking a sip of his Pepsi as he pushed aside some wiring inside Xander's computer to get a better look at the RAM chips. "Extra toasty by the looks of things."

"That's great. Terrific. Your opinion is duly noted. I have noted it, tagged it, and filed it away in my brain under 'advice my idiot friends give me on subjects they

Ignorance is Bliss

know nothing about.' Believe me, I will soon take it into consideration. Whoo-boy, you don't wanna be around when I take this into consideration. It'll be a big-ol' consideration party. Considerate people will come from miles in every direction. They'll eat considerate chips and drink considerate beer and they'll considerably consider considering the information that you so considerably gave to me," Xander said, all in one breath, never once looking up as he used a small blade to slice the ends off of some computer wire.

"You know, a man can overdose on sarcasm," Mike drawled, stroking his statically fluffed blonde hair. He was topless, having taken off his sweater a few moments ago before examining the computer's internals. There was an old scar on his right side with dots all around it, indicating where stitches had been.

Xander chuckled, nodding before looking up at his friend. "Hey!" he yelled, raising an arm to quickly point at his friend's Pepsi. "No drinks near the computer!"

"But it's thirsty."

"You're an idiot. You'll drink near it, and yet you'll take off your shirt to avoid static. Unbelievable."

"Maybe I just wanted to take my shirt off," he grinned mischievously.

Xander shot him a look. "That's funny. Thanks anyway, but I happen to have a date tonight."

"Who's the lucky fella?" Mike laughed, ignoring Xander's previous order and taking another sip of his cola, making sure that he saw.

Again, Xander glared at him, even as he reconnected the computer wire to the newly installed RAM chips, letting the machine hum to life. "Success," he smiled happily. "And, for your information, it is a girl, dumbass."

"Gee, he looks like Xander," Mike said to an imaginary person next to him. "But he talks in a funny, non-Xander-speak kind of way."

Xander turned on the screen. In the same motion he picked up a can of cologne and spritzed himself with it, ignoring Mike's commentary on the subject.

"How is Julie?" Mike asked finally, taking the hint. "She doing all right?"

Xander started unbuttoning the grease stained green shirt that he always used when he was working on electronics. Several of the buttons were ripped out, but he still did the motion of undoing them anyway, like a preprogrammed action. He whipped the smelly shirt off of his back and tossed it into the corner, revealing a back covered in scars.

Every time he saw them, they served to remind Mike that nothing was as it should be. That nothing was safe, not really.

"She's fine, I guess," Xander answered, spreading some deodorant underneath his arms, wincing as unclosed wounds got stretched to the point that the tender flesh began to rip.

"You guess?" Mike scoffed, waving a finger at Xander. "Come on, we both know better than that. Every time I say her name, you get all glossy-eyed... plus, those pants are tight. You don't need to be jumping off the walls for me to know you're excited."

Xander squirted blue gel out of a slender round bottle, slowly turning and raising an eyebrow at Mike. "You're weird," he informed his friend coolly.

"And you're homophobic," Mike chipped in, taking a squirt of gel himself and ruffling it through his golden bangs, giving him that straight-from-the-shower look that he was sure would go over well with the ladies.

"That's great. Terrific. Your opinion is duly noted. I have noted it, tagged it, and filed it away in my brain under 'advice my idiot friends - "

"Okay! I get it." Mike snapped, giving his friend a little shove. "Jesus, I never met anyone so frigging hooked on the same few gags. I swear by all that's holy, Leno changes his act more than you do."

"Funny."

"I try."

Xander finished gelling his hair, turning it from being simply dark to pitch black. Now it was nearly down in front of his eyes, hiding his bushy eyebrows. Someone had once told him that he had the eyebrows of a Sasquatch, although he couldn't quite recall who at the moment. Probably that Canadian kid.

Mike took a moist towelette off the dresser and started using it to scrub the sleep from underneath his eyes, along with the rest of his big-cheeked, freckled face. Still shirtless, he was left vulnerable when Xander reached over casually and pinched him on the arm. "Ow!"

"Wimp."

"Pinching. The last defense of a loser."

"I thought that was screaming?"

"Fine then. The second last defense of a loser."

"Where do crotch shots go in the grand scheme of things?"

"You may now shut up."

"Oh, then I guess I shall, Master." Xander bowed, using the same motion to pick up a burgundy shirt with Chinese symbols on it off the floor. "What do you think of this?"

Mike gave the shirt a once over, and then Xander. "Dude... you're a woman."

"Sexist pig."

"Yeah, what of it?" Mike retorted, grabbing the shirt and putting it on. He was bigger than Xander, so the shirt was tighter on him, and he couldn't button it up as far. He grinned at his reflection in Xander's small, cracked mirror.

"How come when I wear it I'm a woman, but you think you can pull it off?"

"Because I'm secure enough in my masculinity to look man-pretty no matter what I have on. You, on the other hand, should stick to black."

"Why black?"

"It's your colour."

"It's not even a colour."

"Sure it is."

"It's the absence of colour."

"Fine. Then it's your absence of colour."

"Wish you were absent," Xander grumbled, picking up a black shirt and pulling it on over his head. The result was a slim, stream-lined Xander. Everything about him, his clothes, hair, eyes... all jet black. It made his skin look extra pale, but worked well on him. "When you're right, you're right, though," he agreed, grabbing a smoke off his computer table and resting it between his lips, lighting it.

"You smoke in the house now?" Mike frowned, stepping away as the disgusting scent of nicotine reached him.

"Mom found out. Doesn't care. They smoke, too, so we just end up bummin' off one another anyway."

"One big, happy, cancerous family."

"I've never wanted to live forever anyway." Xander smirked, taking a long drag and inhaling deeply, holding it in for ten seconds, then slowly exhaling. "Heaven."

"You're dumb."

"I so do not care right now. Besides, you're starting to sound like Cathy."

There was a pause then, as both men took in what was said and let it register.

"How is she?" Xander asked, sighing as he avoided eye contact by searching for socks.

"Better. She's talking to me, a little anyway. We're going to the dance together tonight, at least."

"I feel like it's my fault."

"No way," Mike protested, standing up. "There was no way you could have known. No way you could have stopped what was happening. It was my fault. If I'd been more careful, she never would have been in that situation."

Xander paused, looking at his friend. Tears were welling up in the man's eyes, making their blue shimmer and shake. When Xander finally spoke, he chose his words very carefully.

"That's the way I used to talk about it," he started, taking a deep breath. "'It happens.' 'She never would have.' Always keeping myself out of the story just enough that I wouldn't have to realize that it happened to me."

He paused, taking another puff of his cigarette and letting the smoke from it curl around his head.

"But it did happen to me. Just like this new thing happened to you. It seems really long ago, doesn't it? Like it didn't even happen. Like it's a story you tell, not even real. But it was real. It happened."

"Tell me," Mike pleaded, grabbing Xander's arm to stop him from turning away.

Xander looked him up and down, then nodded. "You know most of it. Back when me, you, Sara and Cathy thought we had it rough. When we thought that the world was against us. Really, we were just kids. I guess someone a lot older and smarter than me might say that all teens are supposed to feel that way, but it doesn't change the fact."

He doused his cigarette, immediately grabbing another from the pack and placing it between his lips, struck a match, and lit it.

"We were idiots. We should have enjoyed what we had, but we weren't even bright enough to realize we had it. Then, one day, we lost our whole world."

"The day Jamie died," Mike finished softly, looking down for a moment. Jamie Dawkins had been his best friend for years, and the first victim in a long and violent string of murders that swept through their quiet eastern Maine town.

"That was the day we lost one thing, and one thing only: the illusion. The thought that everything was alright. We tell ourselves that it was the loss of our friend, but it wasn't. It was the realization that life wouldn't always be

Ignorance is Bliss

the same. That we weren't safe, and never had been.

"Sara took it hardest, Jamie's death drove her right into my arms... right where I wanted her to be, coincidentally. She and I came closer to being together than we had in the fifteen years before it in those few days. Forged bonds that'll never break.

"That was why she was the next to go. Genblade took her, when everything caved in. When Grendel tried to rape Cathy. When Julie told Derek about how she'd been taken advantage of... everything happened in those few moments. That was why nobody was looking, when Adam Genblade slid his blade deep into her gut."

"I know all this," Mike said impatiently. "What happened afterward? What happened at Engen?"

Xander took a long drag of his smoke, weighing out the pros and cons of finishing the story. "I met a man named Abner Jenkins. He was the commander of the Alpha Strike Force, the first and most deadly wave of Engen's elite guardsmen back in the day. Until my mother escaped trying to rescue me. I was a part of operation: Black Womb. The project to create the world's first post-human child.

"I was a failure. I didn't carry what they called the Darkness, or so they thought. My mother rescued me, and it cost her life... but it took Jenkins' as well.

"He was a walking corpse. Had been bathed in chemical residue from all the containment pods in Engen. He'd stayed alive all those years, under the tutelage of the founders of the company, learning, creating genetic soldiers."

"Genblade and Spider," Mike breathed, rubbing the

flesh between his eyes.

"The genetic Adam and Eve. But they were unstable internally, much like Jenkins himself. All three needed human organs to survive. Adam and Spider could take them, they were engineered for such processes, but Abner..."

"He needed a catalyst."

"...me. Or, the part of me that was thought a failure. The Womb, lying dormant deep inside me for all these years. They woke it up, used it to help them kill all my friends, family, Sara... everything. And then, he offered to take it from me, to keep him alive and to keep me from killing."

"You had the chance to give it up?"

"And I did. Freely, willingly. But Abner lied. He was going to use the darkness to survive the coming Armageddon... a nuclear apocalypse he himself would start. I had to stop him. So, I fought my way through. Killed Spider, stopped Genblade... and took back what was mine from Jenkins."

"To save everything," Mike sighed, shaking his head.

"But even after that, the Womb still kept killing. It's only the last few weeks I've been able to manage any level of control. And that's what I would tell myself, just like you are now: it kept killing. Like this thing is separate from me. It's as much me as any other part. I was born with it, I'll probably die with it. I killed those people. I'm responsible for Sara's death. It's only now that I can say it. So, Mike, what are you detaching yourself from?"

Mike stopped, taken aback. He looked at Xander with betrayed disgust, which he returned with a stone cold face, awaiting response. His lower lip quivered, as tears returned to his eyes. "My child died. I was going to have a child..." Tears began to fall down his face, and he collapsed to his knees.

Xander took hold of the back of his friend's head, pulling him into his chest and holding his close, letting wave after wave a grim realization find the man he considered a brother.

"Gawd, it was my child..." he gasped, drowning on his sorrow as his lungs fought for breath.

"My child..."

୵✕ブ

Mike's cute, but he's got definite issues. There's no doubt he's got a dark side. People think I don't get that, but really, I get it more than anyone. I've seen it, up close and personal, and it isn't pretty... but doesn't every man have a little beast inside of him?

Cathy and Mike are still going through the rough spot to end all rough spots. They think it's, like, world ending, but I've seen this same thing a hundred times before and they're just being stupid about it. Cathy got pregnant. No big surprise there, I just wonder if it was Mike's. Someone should tell her that if you're going to give it up so easy, you have to wear a rubber. Or at least have some kind of protection. Maybe I'm giving the her too much credit. But I thought Mike would know better, somehow.

Anyway, so Cathy's pregnant, but then she's just not. She has a miscarriage, like, right in the middle of school, like some kind of spaz. But, anyway, now she's not pregnant.

Suddenly, it's all 'poor Mike, poor Cathy' when they're not even, like, together anymore as far as anyone can tell. I guess they're still an item, but how long can that really last? They should just break up and get it over with.

Xander, he's another story.

Nobody really knows what's up with him, but he seems to know what's going on with everybody else. It's seriously creepy sometimes, the way that it happens. Sometimes, he'll just know things. It's like he goes home at night and spends all his time calling everyone in town to find out everything that's going on. But most times, the stuff he knows is stuff nobody would tell. Like when him and Mike helped take down that guy that hurt Julie, Xander just knew stuff. He knew where to be to help Cathy... as if she wasn't just giving it up anyway.

But what's really creepy is when you tell him stuff. You tell him secrets you shouldn't tell anyone, things that could get you killed. I don't know why, but every time I have something big happening, I always tell him first. I always check in with him, just to let him know that everything's fine. I dunno, it's stupid, he's a total social reject... but sometimes he's the best one of us. Sometimes you have to tell him things, because he's the guy that always wants to hear it, always wants to help.

I've been around a lot of guys, and they always look at me like I'm nothing. Which fits, because that's what I am. Why else would those guys down the block have got it in their head? But even when he's with girls like me and Julie and Cathy, he doesn't look at us like he wants us. Doesn't look at me like I'm a slut. He just... looks at me, and I tell him everything, and then everything is all right.

There aren't many guys like that.

⋏⋏⋏

The room was large, easily twice the size of the room of the average kid in his class. It was lined with pictures of his life. That had always been a yearly ritual of Tommy's. Every year, he'd change all of the pictures on his wall to those he'd taken the year before. His family had always called him shutterbug for it back when they paid any attention to him at all.

The past year was documented on those walls, each frame glistening in the beam from the pull-string light hanging from his ceiling, a testament to how old the house really was.

Cameras, film, frames... That's what most people gave him for gifts. Not that he minded. It was his one real hobby, and he loved it. Last year, someone had been smart enough to give him a bulk film loader, cutting his costs drastically. Over in the corner was his closet, converted into a makeshift darkroom. There were always clothes on his floor with nowhere to hang them.

The photos on the wall told the story of the most interesting parts of his life. This year, when everything is supposed to change for young men and women, everything changed. Only for them, it was different.

He pulled on an old tee-shirt and turned to face one of the photos. It had been taken in the Factory, a place that had died off in the few months since. It was like he was the only person who had time for it anymore. In the picture was Cathy, Mike, and Jamie all leaning against a pool table. Mike and Jamie had their arms crossed, trying to look tough, while Cathy tried her best to hide her face from the camera.

There was another picture of Sud, Jamie, Derek, Mike

and himself taken just a few months later. Grendel had taken it, he thought. There they were: the Avengers, the Squadron Supreme, the Teen Titans. It had always been the five of them, ever since they were kids. Xander had never fit into it. Most of his photos of Xander were lone shots. He was always either talking to Sara or watching gay porn on the internet or something.

There was a picture of Sara and Grendel kissing, back when the two of them had been an item. They both looked so happy, her hair was so gorgeous...

There was another picture of a long line of headstones. Their headstones were front and center, Julian Grendel and Sara Johnson, buried very near to one another. He always thought it was poetic that the two of them had died on the same day. It should be that way, when two people are meant for each other like that. It was beautiful. Sure, at the time, Grendel had been with Cathy and Sara had been going after Jamie, but that didn't change the fact that they would have gotten together. He liked to think that they were together now.

Then there was the picture that was flipped around, facing the wall. That was the one he wanted so badly to take down, but was afraid to. It was a head shot of Derek Smith, his steel blue eyes staring right into the camera, making them look like they focused on you no matter where you were in the room. Eyes that made Tommy wonder how they'd ever thought Derek was okay. How they hadn't known that he was a murderer. The eyes... they made him look as though he would jump out of the page and start ripping into you if he could. Maybe he'd use that knife he carried around, the one they used to teased him about, saying that he'd never used it. That he looked stupid. That was why the picture was flipped over. He was too afraid to take it down, too afraid it would piss Derek off.

There were other pictures, too. Ones that would never come down. Pictures of Jamie, Grendel, Sud, Sara... all of them dead. All of them killed senselessly, violently. Ripped open for all to see.

He pulled on some black jeans, then sprayed himself with a bottle of cheap aerosol cologne to mask any of the excess funk.

Now he was the only one left. Sometimes he thought the loneliness would kill him. Other times he hoped it would. Maybe then he'd see them again, maybe then he'd find peace.

He turned to his mirror and checked his hair once again to make sure that the gel was holding every spike in place perfectly. Rubbing a hand over his recently shaven face, he smiled brightly at the mirror, choosing to not be lonely anymore tonight. He turned and looked at his newest picture, one of Julie, Mandy, Mike, Cathy and Xander, and smiled warmly at it. If the world he lived in was changing, then maybe it was time for him to change with it.

᚛᚜

Tommy's kinda like the Lone Ranger now. He's got nobody, and I feel bad for him. First Jamie dies, then Grendel, then Sud dies and all his other friends try stuff with me, and now they're all on the run, so if he does see them, it's in a poorly lit alley.

Maybe that's where he met Cathy. Seems like the type of

place she'd hang out.

Ever since that thing in the hospital a week ago when Julie and Xander hooked up (finally), things have been stressed between everyone else. Mike and Cathy are still together, even though they're never in the same room. So now, everybody's waiting for me and Tommy to either get together or pair off with different people ourselves. Suddenly it's like, not okay to be single and loving it anymore. Now we gotta talk to people between make out sessions.

It blows entirely.

It wouldn't even be so bad if Mike and Cat would just hurry up and end it or whatever.

ᚲ ᚱ

Cathy winced as she poked a faux-diamond earring through the hole in her ear, gritting her teeth a little as she did so.

It had been months since she had had any reason to wear earrings, or jewelry of any kind for that matter (although from time to time she was prone to slipping on her mother's pearl necklace to go to school, just for the sake of showing off a little bit). In her season-long period of social hibernation, she didn't realize that the flesh had folded and grown over the punctures in each lobe, which she had had since before she was old enough to walk.

Now she hissed as pain shot through the side of her head, staring at her reflection in her bathroom mirror and trying desperately to keep her hair out of her line of sight. As her teeth clenched together, she cursed on herself for being so weak. After all she'd been through, this should be nothing. This *was* nothing. After all the pain and sorrow and heartache... after all of the times that she thought agony would keep bleeding from her heart until she was dead, a small piece of metal through each earlobe shouldn't have even fazed her.

And yet she squinted her eyes until they were shut and bit her lip with two paper-white teeth, trying to plunge the earring through the tender skin. Anguish jolted through her system and forced her to pull back at the last second, unable to take it any longer.

"Fuck," she said, glancing in the mirror and wanting to strike out at what she saw there, even going so far as to clench a tight little fist.

Instead her knuckles loosened. She pulled back her neatly combed black hair, revealing the tiniest dribbles of blood, pushed out through the dent in her head by the pressure from her heart.

"Argh!" she huffed as quietly as possible, mindful of her parents and sister downstairs. She ran her fingers through her hair and dug her long nails into her scalp until she thought it might bleed as well.

She bent over and picked up the earring, her lower back aching from weeks of restless nights and uncomfortable, lonely trips to the doctor's office. Calcium popped in her hip, making her blink once in surprise before coming back up to stand, the earring pinched between her thumb and forefinger.

Holding it up to the row of incandescent light bulbs that surrounded her bathroom mirror, she noticed a small, swirling splotch of blood on the cubic zirconia. It made the light that reflected off of it a sickly, dark red. Her free hand automatically went to her ear, returning with the smallest possible dot of blood on it.

She remembered those commercials. *A diamond is forever*, they always said at the end, while the two shadows were kissing happily and holding one another. She wondered who those people were. Were they really happy? Or was there something else going on there?

Maybe the shadow-couple had been having problems lately, bad ones. The guy was an idiot and would rather talk to his idiot friends about his problems, leaving the girl at home all alone. Then, of course, the guy would come back home drunk at four in the morning expecting to get lucky, but no, the girl doesn't want to obviously. So, he goes for the easy fix. Instead of talking the problems out, he saves up and buys her a diamond ring. She is filled with fleeting, momentary gratification and the false impression that their problems are solved, they make love, go maybe a week without incident, and are finally back where they started.

The commercial should say: 'A Diamond: it'll open her knees,' she thought.

But still, before her was a tiny piece of treated glass with a swirling puddle of red in it. She stared at it intently, at the way the light spun out of it like a spider web, or that CD cover from that one old British band about bricks and drugs. If she looked hard enough, the redness seemed to dance for her, painting a macabre tapestry of what she had to look forward to in her life. She reached out without looking, without thinking, and turned on the bathroom sink. She shoved the earring under it, watching as the swirls of red melted off, danced around against the white of the sink for a moment, then disappeared down the drain.

When she returned the small trinket to her sight, she could still see the red. It wasn't there, she knew it couldn't be, but she was convinced that she could see it. She stuck it underneath the running water again, the cold of it nipping at her slender fingers, sending tiny shocks up her arm. She felt the blood pump to the chilled appendages, and the pores in her flesh became visible as some of her recently applied nail polish traveled down the sink as well. She pulled back the earring again, looked at it only a second, then put it back beneath the flow.

This was not the first time in the past week that Cathy had been forced to wash out tiny droplets of blood. They had been found decorating the inside of silk undergarments of late, along with bed sheets, jeans, and the occasional pair of pajamas. It wasn't her cycle, she knew that much. They were too irregular. Wrong time for it too, even though recent events might have thrown her off course.

She knew what it was. It was her child still inside of her, screaming for something she could not hear. She could picture it, wriggling about within her, wanting food or water and getting nothing, her bleeding from the inside out the only indication of her unborn child's anguish.

And so, Cathy Kennessy had become accustomed to a schedule which included the late night to early morning washing of sheets and scrubbing of mattresses, and the feeling of cold water freezing the tips of her fingers as redness washed down the drain.

Out, out, damn spot.

She withdrew the earring again. It was almost clean now, only the slightest hint of pink where the blood had been. Pink was a colour that she was more readily pre-pared to contend with. She poked the freezing cold metal through her ear now without hesitation, then the other, and mechanically flipped open her makeup kit and start-ed to apply foundation.

The dance tonight is like the sudden rush of air after you've been holding your breath underwater for a really long time. You wait for it, you ache for it, and even though you know it's go-ing to hurt just a little, it's outweighed by feeling so good. The people around here though, they don't seem to think so.

Coral Beach is weirder than any place I've ever been to, even though nobody seems to realize it. Everyone in this town feels like they're, like, waiting for the other Wal-Mart reject shoe to suddenly drop.

Social gatherings are the worst.

Apparently a while back some dude went all Freddy at a party around here, all hack-and-slash and stuff. Since then, ev-eryone's got cabin fever, and not the cool kind from Muppet Treasure Island, either. The kind that makes everyone turn into social lepers and stay inside all the time, like there's something in the dark that's going to jump out and bite them.

Xander was really interested in going. He saw the poster up in school when he was walking around with Julie and had been all: 'Hell - yes.' He actually smiled, a serious rarity, but it's becoming more common than a lot of people realize.

The teachers weren't so happy 'cause they have to chaperone. Apparently the students aren't the only people with house-rat syndrome. The only one that jumped at the chance was Principal Schneider, and the rest of them had to be bullied into it. I don't think Mr. Miles was all too pleased about it, he said something in that Boston accent of his about today's music sounding like the musicians played their guitars with rabid cats.

Julie didn't want to go at first, which is the opposite of everything she's been since she was eight. But the second she saw that Xander... sorry! Alexander... wanted to go, she was all over it (and him), which is more like the Julie we all know and tolerate.

Cathy didn't want to go. She still doesn't, I think. She's just dragging herself along to make an appearance. She'll show up long enough to be like, 'Hey, look everyone, Mike's still my boyfriend,' then she'll go home with the first piece of raw meat she can find and won't be seen for a few days.

Mike wanted to go really bad. Him and Xander were practically dancing around like little girls when they saw the poster. But, as usual, one look from Cathy took the smile right off his face and buried it next to Alicia Silverstone's career. He was brought right back down to the dumps, and when he went to her, she turned away and left. Poor her. Wah. I so totally feel her pain. Right.

But still, most of the other kids scoffed at the poster. It's like it's not in style to have fun in this town anymore. They need to get out and relax. I mean, sure, after what happened with the Tee's I dress a little more conservative, but I still go out. You can be careful without being a reject.

Nothing's going to happen tonight anyway.

CHAPTER TWO:
NOTHING WRONG

He sat in the bushes.

In his mind, that was all he was doing, and there was nothing wrong with that.

Just off of where Morrison Drive intersected with Quesada Way, he was sitting in the bushes, peering out between windswept late fall branches at the street before him, following the odd leaf that the wind blew into his line of sight.

His hand was on his crotch, massaging it rhythmically, and he bit his lip as he felt himself near climax.

Don't do that, Malcolm.

Someone told him in a stern voice deep within his subconscious. He squinted his eyes, forcing the voice out. He couldn't recall who the voice was, only that he hated it, shrill and loud. It made his ears hurt. His vision became spotty momentarily as he felt pleasure build inside him, coupled with just the right amount of pain to make it last. Make it interesting. He bent forward, opening his mouth to speak and then shut it, afraid of who would hear, afraid of the voice that was telling him to stop.

Don't do that, Malcolm.

"Shut up, bitch," he whispered to himself, and the voice continued to speak, fading now. He was confronted by the image of a shovel, but it passed as quickly as it came.

He leaned forward again, brushing against the orange and yellow leaves, so good against his face.

"Mmm."

He loved this time of year, loved the chill that the air brought with it. Colours were everywhere, leaves were randomly different shades and textures, as though some-one had taken out a box of crayons and coloured them without rhyme or reason.

He'd rented a dirty movie from the corner store earlier and paid the overweight man at the counter five dollars for it. The old, used paper bill had felt like leaves in his palm as he handed it over, tucking the porno under his arm and smiling at the woman who walked in through the front door, shying her children away from him. He'd smiled at the children too and they'd waved at him. He waved back.

The movie had not been overly satisfying. It was ripe with the plotting efforts of a bad writer unable to accept the reality of his place in life, that people who rent pornog-raphy are not in the least bit interested in what the charac-ters are feeling, unless what they are feeling is something long and nasty. He had only attempted masturbating to it for a moment, until the voice had said, *Don't do that, Malcolm.*

"Shut up."

But the flick wasn't good enough. There were no blondes in it, and he couldn't get himself into it enough that the voice would stop. So he'd stopped and taken a walk into the woods outside his house, wrapping a scarf around his neck so that he wouldn't get cold. He'd been walking for about a half hour when he peered out from between the branches and saw a young couple walking. The girl had blonde hair that fell all the way down to the swell of her buttocks, and the boyfriend's hand had been upon it.

Malcolm felt himself rise in a way that the porno had not produced and knelt down in the mulch and dying grass, the dampness at his knees feeling surprisingly good. Then the voice said,

Don't do that, Malcolm.

But he told the bitch to shut up and it went away as quickly as it had come, so he decided to stay. Maybe the wind was drowning her out and that was why he couldn't hear her. In any event, he hadn't planned this, he wasn't like that, so there was nothing wrong with it.

He wiped sweat off of his balding head with his free hand, pumping more fiercely to increase the pressure and the pleasure, hoping that climax would come before nightfall. He watched another girl go by, a redhead (not as good as a blonde, but still better than brunettes). She had a rather large chest, and it bounced as she walked. She stopped a few feet to the left of his vision, looking around to assure herself that there was nobody about then reached into the back of her jeans and fixed her cotton thong.

"Mmm," he said, and there was nothing wrong with that, as he watched her bend over to tie her shoe lace, showing off her full, grab-worthy backside just for him, then walked on.

She knew that he was there, he decided. Some of the others that walked down Morrison didn't know, but she definitely did. She didn't want to have sex with him, he had no delusions of that, but she wanted to show off for him. To aid in his pleasure without having the guilt that comes to young girls that sleep with older men. So she showed him what she wanted to and had moved on, and later, when night fell and her parents were asleep, she would slide her hands below her red covers and think of the man in the bushes, stroking himself to her short peep show, and there was nothing wrong with that.

Don't do that, Malcolm.

"Shut up!" he whispered again, closing his eyes tight and gritting his teeth. When he opened them again he saw a teenage blonde finish her escape from his vision. She had been wearing a skirt, and possibly could have bent over. The voice had made him miss it.

Maybe he could go through the woods a little ways, get in front of her. Maybe she would have an itch and need to bend again and want him to see, like the other

Don't do that, Malcolm.

"Quiet, bitch!" he said, releasing his grip and punching a tree to show that he was serious. "I said shut up and now you're going to shut up. So shut up!"

He waited in the approaching twilight for the voice to come back. It did not. He smiled a little, then reached down again... to feel only softness.

Not the smooth, hard thing that the redhead with the thong wanted to dream about late at night. He sneered, tucking it away and rising to his feet above the bushes, then turned to walk back home.

"What ya doin'?" came the sound, small and tender, with just a touch of childish spite.

Malcolm turned and saw him, walking down Morrison Street toward Quesada Way. The child was no more than ten, probably nine, and only stood as tall as Malcolm's waist. And there was nothing wrong with that.

He wore a black and red tee-shirt with a stain on it, and jeans bought at the local market by his mother.

And his hair.

It was short with small curls at the tips that said mother had tried to get out, so blond that it was nearly white.

"What ya doing?" the child repeated.

Malcolm smiled warmly, as he finished zipping himself up. "I'm just out for a walk."

"You walk in the woods?"

"Yes. It's fun."

"Oh," the child responded. "Okay."

"What are you doing?" Malcolm asked.

The child looked hesitant. "Mom sent me down to the store to get some bread, and a candy for me."

Malcolm thought of the obese man at the store that had sold him the badly written porno. He would not appreciate such a magnificent child.

"I have bread at home I can give you," he said politely. "And lots of candy, not just one."

"Is your house in the woods?"

"No, but that's how we'll get there."

"Mom says I'm not allowed in the woods."

"But your mom wants you to get bread, and I have the

bread. So she wouldn't mind."

The child considered that for a moment, thoughts of candy flying through his young mind. "Okay."

He reached out and took the child's small hand, leading him past the brush and into the woods. "I'm Malcolm, what's your name?"

"Charles. Charles Frank."

"Hello, Charles Frank."

"Hello, Malcolm."

Don't do that, Malcolm.

"Shut up."

"What?"

"Nothing."

He led the boy away from the road and deep into the woods toward his home. He hadn't planned on this, and the boy wanted to come.

There was nothing wrong with it.

CHAPTER THREE:
THE DANCE

Julie and Mandy Peterson walked into the gym of Coral Beach High, both wishing immediately that the dance had been held at The Factory or some location where the school losers were not always in charge of decoration.

Fall-coloured orange, red, and yellow streamers stretched across the ceiling. At some point they had run out of orange and had started using bright purple instead, making something already gaudy into a design nightmare. Other 'fall' decorations including pumpkins, scarecrows and witches left over from the canceled Halloween dance, even though Halloween was a month ago.

There was a disco ball... yes, a disco ball positioned to hang from the middle of the gym, with orange, red and blue lights aimed at it, bouncing their reflection in all directions. The beams of light shimmered off of the body paint that spotted Julie's tight black pants and raggedy, red sleeveless shirt, and did nothing but create unflattering shadows on Mandy's sweater.

"I still can't believe you wore that," Julie scoffed between her teeth, her eyes still scanning the crowd.

"Would you drop it?" Mandy said passively as she scanned the crowd herself, her eyes darting this way and that. "I bought this just last week. It looks alright. You look just weird, dressing like that when it's this cold out."

Julie balked, looking at her cousin for just a moment. She opened her mouth to speak, then closed it and turned away to ignore her again. She decided that she actually would drop it, for now.

Across the gym Xander stood up, his black leather coat unbunching as he rose. His hands were concealed by sleeves too long for them, making his arms appear shorter than they actually were. He smiled warmly and checked his red shirt and blue jeans (he had decided against Mike's choice of black on black) to make sure there was nothing on them, then started to walk forward. He gave a little wave, then turned to Mike (who was sitting beside him) and motioned for him to rise as well.

Mike did so, reluctantly, and the two navigated the mingling teenagers on the dance floor.

"Here they come," Julie smiled, turning to Mandy. "Try not to be a spaz around Mike, okay?"

Mandy gave a fake, condescending grin in return. "Try to wait until you're out of public view to accidentally lose your shirt, okay?"

Julie frowned, then turned back toward the oncoming boys. "Hey guys," she said sheepishly to both of them, although it was clear that the plural was only for politeness and that she was only talking to Xander.

"Hey," Xander replied, reaching out and pulling her into a little hug, leaving Mike and Mandy to simply nod courteously at one another. Mandy gave a smile, and Mike returned it. "You're a little late."

Julie grinned devilishly, relishing in the fact that her arms were wrapped around his neck. "You have a lot to learn about women, Mr. Drew. Don't you know that it's fashionable to arrive at least ten minutes later than you're supposed to?"

"Silly me," he chuckled, slowly releasing his hold on her hips, sliding his hands across her exposed skin and sending shivers up and down her spine that passed on to him. "I thought maybe you just liked to see me squirm."

She giggled, and it sounded odd. Usually with her it was an all out laugh, not the cute, kitteny sound that now bubbled from her vocal cords. "That too," she replied.

Mike forced a little smile as he turned and glanced around, trying not to notice their exchange. "Maybe that's what Cathy's doing. If so, it's really working."

"Maybe she's not coming." Mandy shrugged, smiling in an effort to make the comment sound innocent.

Mike turned, his brow furrowed.

"What?" he asked, not angry but shocked.

"Well, that, like, wouldn't totally break with her character lately...really."

Mike's eyes lost what little glow they had left, and he turned toward the tiled floor, which was painted for its use in basketball.

"No," he reluctantly agreed. "I guess it wouldn't."

Xander turned to his friend and smiled. "And it certainly wouldn't break with her character to show up looking astonishing just as you started to doubt her."

"What?"

Xander motioned behind Mike to the rear doors.

He turned and Cathy was there, her hair straight and shining, with sparkling earrings on and her mother's pearl necklace draped around her slender neck. She wore a faded, tight yellow tee-shirt and a long, slinky orange skirt. She matched the fall theme so perfectly that it seemed like the dance had been designed for her.

"See?" Julie whispered, nudging Mandy. "There's a girl who knows how to dress for the occasion."

�ↄⱷↄ

Tommy danced in traditional teenage guy fashion, shuffling his feet a little from side to side and pumping a fist in the air when the people around him started to. Not too far from him, Mike, Xander, and the girls sat the dance out.

Cathy was one empty chair away from Mike, a distance that felt like miles rather than inches.

"So, how's the Coral Beach nightlife treating you?" Xander asked, turning toward Mandy and giving her a grin.

She turned to him, surprised at the sudden sound of his voice above the roaring thump of the music. The look faded into a grin not that different from his own, her natural features showing how beautiful she could be when there wasn't a pound of makeup weighing her down. "This is all right," she mumbled, fumbling her feet beneath her chair.

"What?" Xander asked, raising a hand to his ear as Julie squeezed the other one on his leg possessively.

"I said, this is all right," Mandy repeated, her voice

raised above the bump of the bass.

Xander gave her a thumbs up, proving that nonverbal communication worked best at a dance. "How come you didn't bring a date? I hear that Evan guy in your class likes you."

Mandy scrunched up her nose and giggled a little. Her feet came back from beneath her chair as she loosened up. "Evan? He's such a little freakazoid. Yesterday in Family Living class, he totally weirded out when the teacher started talking all sex ed."

Xander frowned. "I can relate to the guy. Getting lectured on sex by a forty-year-old virgin isn't the most relaxing thing in the world. Has she shown you the pictures of the STI's yet?"

Mandy's eyes grew wide. "Um, no."

"Skip class tomorrow," he advised in a sage tone, patting her on the shoulder.

"No problem," she assured him, nodding readily, eyes still wide.

Xander smiled. She was cute, in a youthful way. She reminded him of someone right at that moment, but he couldn't quite put his finger on who. Julie squeezed his hand again, and he turned toward her, giving Mandy one last little smile.

"That was nice," Julie smiled honestly, taking both his hands in hers now. He didn't even realize she had done it, it felt so natural.

"What?"

"You talking to her like that. I haven't seen her loosen up like that since we brought her home."

"All I did was talk with her. You don't mind, do

you?"

Julie laughed. "Not at all. It's cute. It's nice that you're nice to her."

"Nicely said."

"Nice of you to say so."

He laughed, unable to think of another way to use the word 'nice', thereby losing their verbal match. She pointed at him, calling him on it, and he produced a defeated look in acknowledgment.

She laughed again, and the orange rays reflecting off the disco ball got caught in her hair, making her glimmer with life and youth, her eyes sparkling with happiness.

Mandy watched them for a moment, wondering if Xander would turn back to talk to her. It wasn't that she felt left out, just that she didn't want to be otherwise engaged if the conversation had not been over. After a minute, she turned toward Mike on the other side of her. "So, what's up with the empty chair? Waiting for someone?"

Mike turned to her, as if just noticing that she was there. "Huh? No... just being comfortable. Me and Cat both appreciate our leg room."

She shot him a skeptical look.

"You get into those things when you've been with someone long enough. It's instinct," he assured her, although it was clear that she was anything but assured.

"Uh-huh," she said in a chipper voice, then nudged herself a little closer to him.

Mike looked down at the shrinking distance between them, then back at her. "What are you doing?"

"Nothing," she said truthfully, her legs ducking back between her chair. "You make me feel, like, safer, is all."

He nodded slowly, feeling like a heel for calling the younger girl out on her obvious crush.

"Oh," he said. "That's okay, then."

Someone went up to the DJ, and the music slowly changed pace. Apparently someone else was sick of hearing the same two words in a successive beat for twenty minutes every song.

The twang of an electric guitar slowly being played was followed by the coos of girls all over the gymnasium as they realized what song it was, each of them either grabbing their boyfriends or the nearest available guy.

"Tears in Heaven!" Julie said longingly, turning to Xander. "I really love this song."

Xander turned, observing the dance floor. "Apparently a lot of people do. Don't you think it's a bit crowded?"

She smiled, stroking the end of his chin lightly. "I only see you."

With that he rose, taking her by the hand and leading her to a spot on the dance floor where not too many people were and placed his hands low around her hips, latching together around her backside as she did the same around his neck. They looked into each other's eyes as they moved, glancing away only long enough to smile politely at people they knew who danced near them.

Mike turned to Cathy, a grin pushing one freckled cheek up.

"You wanna dance?" he asked softly, looking at her like she was the most radiant thing the world had ever seen.

She frowned, her eyes falling across the dance floor at Xander and Julie, then at everyone else as the lyrics began.

She turned back to her lover and shook her head slowly. "Not really."

"Come on," he coaxed, reaching out and touching her arm softly.

She jerked away as she felt his fingers, a panicked look coming over her. She tried to force it away as she settled back into her position, but he had caught it, along with half the room.

"What the hell?" he breathed, as low as he could. "Cathy, what's going on? You haven't even let me touch you since - "

"Don't," she barked, raising a hand to him. "Don't even try it. I'm not in the mood for this tonight."

"Then what are you in the mood for?" he asked, stretching his arms in question. "'Cause you sure as hell don't ever tell me."

She pursed her lips, then turned away from him. "I just want to be left alone and enjoy the music. Is that okay with you?"

Defeated, he shook his head. "Sure. Listen, I..."

"I don't want to hear it," she snapped, turning away.

He turned away as well, seeing Mandy still beside him, looking at him intently. "Were you just...?"

"No, I wasn't listening," she assured him, backing off a little. "I mean, I heard, but I wasn't..."

"It's okay," he apologized, lifting a hand to wave the accusation away. "Half the gym probably heard that."

There was a long pause, then. Mandy looked around and took off her sweater, revealing a top with a puppy face printed on the chest, then closed the distance between her and Mike yet again. "That wasn't your fault, y'know."

He frowned. "Well, it wasn't hers."

She gave him a disapproving look, but said, "No, I guess not. But you weren't out of line or anything. It's just like you said: it's instinct to do one thing. But your, like, situation's changed a little now, and your instincts tell you to do the wrong things."

He looked up from the floor and smiled at her. "You know... you're brighter than you seem."

She giggled a little. "Come on, I'd have to be."

He laughed at that, and was suddenly at ease again.

"Julie dragged Xander off," she complained, cocking her head toward the pair.

Would you know my name... if I saw you in Heaven?...

"Yeah, he didn't seem too hesitant," Mike chuckled. "Some friends we got, huh?"

"Oh, yeah," she huffed sarcastically. "They really know how to stand by you. Really far to the left, but still technically by you."

Mike huffed. "That's going around lately."

"Ever since I came."

He patted her on the leg, and she shivered. "No. It just seemed that way... truth told, it's been happening for a long time. You're just the first person observant enough to point it out."

She grinned, looked down, took a breath, then turned her head up quickly. "Do you want to dance?"

There was a pause and Mike smiled at the floor. "Mandy, Mandy, Mandy..." he trailed off. "I would be very lucky to dance with you, believe me. But my heart is telling me no..."

He looked at her again, seeing the depressed look on

her face as she began to eye the sweater again.

"But you're right," Mike continued. "Sometimes things change, and you have to do things a new way."

He rose to his feet and extended a hand to her.

She looked up in surprise and wonder. She accepted his hand and stood.

Cathy glared at them, watching them move across the dance floor to a spot opposite Xander and Julie. They put their arms loosely around one another, with about a half foot of distance between.

"Well, that was kinda cold," came a voice from beside Cathy.

She wasn't startled. She didn't even bother to turn her head. "Mike Harris can do what he pleases, Tommy, and so can I."

Tommy shrugged. "I know. It's cool... it just seemed like such a brush off. And Mandy's so into him... it seems like he's just using her to get back at you."

"Maybe you should keep your mouth shut," she suggested, trying hard to lose herself in the music.

He paused a moment, then smiled. "Do you want to dance?"

"What?" she asked, turning to face him again. "You must be crazy. Just because Mike replaced me with a Peterson, that does not mean I'm going to - "

"There's that word."

Cathy sighed. "That's not what I meant."

"You said it, not me. *Replaced*."

Cathy sighed, then smiled.

"You're going through something, I get that. I wasn't trying to be all in-your-face. If you need a fresh set of ears,

I'm here. I know I'm not your friend... but you're mine. One of the only living ones I have left, in fact."

Cathy took his hand and squeezed it. She rolled her eyes, then led him onto the dance floor as the song's beat quickened slightly for the second chorus.

Xander and Julie had gotten steadily closer as the song progressed, and now the two were like spoons, their bodies fitting naturally right next to one another. Julie leaned in, put her head on his shoulder and closed her eyes, letting out a long awaited sigh of complete relaxation. "It's been a long time since I felt like this," she admitted softly, so that only he could hear.

"Is it a good feeling?" he asked, smirking.

"Definitely," she said. He could feel her tiny mouth smile against his red denim shirt.

He was smiling too, he realized. The first true smile he'd experienced in months. Months when nobody, not even his dearest friends, had been this close to him when it wasn't to cry or to shout. To just hold and to be held... he'd almost forgotten what it was like.

"It's like all these doors are opening up to me, to things I haven't let myself feel for so long... does that sound stupid?" she asked, rising from his shoulder to look at him and make sure he wasn't laughing at her secretly.

"No, not at all," he assured her, reaching up and stroking the hair on the back of her head, soft as summer grass between his fingers. "I was just thinking the same thing."

He put gentle pressure on her head, pulling it forward slowly as he leaned in himself, each of their lips quivering with anticipation until they met. They shared each other's warmth in a slow, smooth kiss that felt more right than anything had in a long time. Her lips were silky against his, and his bit of teenage stubble that he refused to shave scratched at her cheeks until they parted, both of them wanting more.

From across the room, Mike watched approvingly from over Mandy's shoulder.

"I'm sorry," Xander said, gasping for breath that had been stolen away. "I'm..."

She leaned in quickly and kissed him again, squeezing his body tight against her own until he began to squeeze too, both of them still faintly aware of the music that played all around them, surrounding them. Consuming them.

"Alex..."

ᚴᚼ

Cathy turned to the beat of the music with Tommy, more joke dancing than anything else. He clasped both of her hands and separated from her slightly, doing a few quick swing dance moves to the Eric Clapton song, getting annoyed and surprised glances from people around them.

She tried to hold it in, then let out a tremendous laugh, letting go of his hands and buckling over.

"See?" he said, breaking into a little disco stance, one hand pointing upward at a fifty-degree angle. "I knew you had one in you somewhere."

She forced herself to stand as she smiled. "You're awful."

"I am. A total scoundrel."

She squinted at him. "No... I thought you would be, but you aren't."

"Oh, gee," he said, pushing out his lower lip and pretending to be hurt. "Thanks a lot."

"I'm serious," she said, tweaking his nose as they began to pretend to waltz, him stepping on her toes every few moves. "This is fun."

"Thank you, ma chère," he said with a cheesy French accent, clenching his teeth as though there was a rose between them. "Now, come back with me to Cuba... we will make beautiful music together, Bay Bee."

She started to laugh again, tapping him on the chest to stop, but he continued.

"In Cuba, you no ride de horse. De horse, my friend, it rides you."

Her laughter was heard all throughout the auditorium, but neither of the pair were anywhere close to caring as it became infectious, consuming him as well.

Mike held Mandy at a distance, and she made no attempt to get closer.

"So, what's on your mind?" she asked passively, smiling at Evan as he glared with the other boys her age on the other side of the gym.

"Absolutely nothing."

She smirked. "Is that why you keep looking at Xander and Jules every time you think I'm not paying any attention?"

"Hey..." Mike smiled. "That's... that's just cheating."

"And we can't forget your looks at Cathy, the girl who didn't feel like dancing."

"Mmm," he agreed. "Good thing she wanted to feel the music, huh?"

"Really."

"Re-ally."

"Re-all-y."

They both started to laugh, and he held her a little tighter. Taking a big chance, she bit her lip and leaned her head forward, resting it on his broad shoulders. He leaned his head against hers, giving her the smallest of pecks on the top of her head as they continued to dance.

He opened his eyes to look around as the music slowed down. "Did you see where Xander and Julie went?"

Beneath the bleachers, in the moonlight that reflected off the football scoreboard, their lips were locked together as if magnetized. Their eyes closed, Julie reached up blindly and pulled his leather jacket off of him, trickling her fingers over his shoulders and chest, smiling in mid-kiss as she did so.

He giggled a little, a sound that seemed foreign coming from him. He pulled her closer by the hips, and she sunk down a little. He followed her until he was almost on top of her, and then they went back up, smiling. Her hair was all around him, like his arms her. Their hearts beat harder and louder than the fast dying Clapton song.

"The music's gone," she said between kisses, as he brought his lips to the curve of her neck playfully.

He stopped, looking so deep into her eyes that he

thought he might drown. "I still hear it."

They kissed again, and continued to do so long into the night, until it was almost time for the dance to end. By the time they got back, almost everyone was gone, and the floor was theirs for one long, amazing dance.

^<^>^

That's the really weird thing about life in Coral Beach.

Mandy wrote as she let down her hair, lying down on her bed when she got back from the dance.

It doesn't matter how bad it gets, there are always going to be places that you can go and know that everything is going to be alright. Like to Xander or Mike, or to a lesser extent, Tommy. They're people who understand what is happening and why, and they have a way of simplifying it and making you believe that life isn't as weird as people make it out to be after all.

CHAPTER FOUR:
THE BOW BREAKS

Los Angeles, California.

She slid through the inch-wide crack in the hardwood floor beneath a stone desk, the black liquid that made up her body bubbling up like boiling, frothy milk. It spread out over the floor and started to spurt up and take shape until curves formed around her hips and breasts, and a sleek, pointed chin came into view. Cute, tiny lips emerged, along with big black eyes that gleamed with childish delight.

Seconds later, Leigh Blackheart was lying in the middle of the floor. Quickly, she stretched her slender neck and peered around the corner of the desk into the long hallway beyond, found it to be vacant, then stood up.

She stretched, took a few deep breaths and wiped the sweat from her brow, then smoothed down her short black hair until it was tight to her scalp. She took a whiff of the air, curled her nose, then looked up at the sign that hung from the ceiling.

Museum of Natural History: The Past is the Way to the

Future.

"I just hope the future doesn't smell this bad," she said, her west coast accent apparent. She turned quickly, scanning the room until she found what she was looking for. In the adjacent room was a tall glass case, inside of which was a blue gem, shimmering in the bright fluorescent lights aimed at it.

Confidently, she walked out into the room and took it in, the smell of old things still following her. She bent over the glass case with an air of sexuality, knowing that she was going to be watched by middle-aged men on security tapes when the deed was done. She read the inscription and smiled coyly to herself.

"The Gem of Aberdean... well, if that isn't a mouthful."

She reached into her pocket and pulled out a glass cutter attached to a large suction cup. She stuck it carefully to the glass, slowly twirling the blade around until a circle had been cut. Softly, she removed the device and tapped the inside of the circle.

Nothing happened.

Sighing, she tapped it again, a little harder.

Again, nothing happened.

"Oh, fuck this," she huffed, reaching back an arm and punching through the glass, shattering the entire case and grabbing the gem as alarms began to sound all around her.

Closing her eyes tightly, her feet began to melt. Her face filled with anguish as the rest of her body followed, and she again disappeared into the floor.

She reemerged a moment later outside the museum,

drenched in sweat. Looking down at the brilliant blue stone in her hand, she smiled devilishly.

"So, you're what everyone's talking about?" she smiled, turning briefly back toward the museum. "Sorry guys. When I collect the five mil for this baby, I'll be sure to send you an air freshener."

Suddenly, she screamed, dropping the gem to the grass.

Her body began to shimmer and shake, blobs boiling off of her everywhere. Even her eyes became as large as dinner plates, then as small as needle-points, as she morphed uncontrollably and fell to the ground.

She turned onto her back, an action that seemed to take all of her energy, and faced her attacker.

There stood a tall, white man with dark brown hair that came down in two long streaks on either side of his face. His face was sharp, almost to the point of being triangular, and his mouth was small and curled up in a holier-than-thou sneer. He wore a strip of cloth across his forehead, which featured a tiny green gem in its center. His eyes were a piercing cobalt blue. The strangest thing about him was his attire. Dressed in long black robes from head to toe that covered his feet and made him look like he was floating, along with patterned pieces of ribbon that twirled about his body, engraved in gold thread with runes and Egyptian symbols. He pointed a long cane at her, and energy crackled from its tip.

If this had been a hundred years ago, she would have said that he was a nobleman.

"Who the fuck are you?" she spat, still twitching, a mixture of blood and sweat seeping from her pores.

"I, am Sebastian LeGaea," he said, making it sound royal and important with his strong Scandinavian accent. "You, are Leigh Blackheart. Formerly Leigh Draco."

He pulled back a leg and kicked her. To her shock, it actually connected.

"You are an idiot. And yet... you have accomplished something I could not, the retrieval of the gem."

"How the hell did you know I was going to be here?"

He looked down at her, raising his cane. "I hired you, you twit. I hate to inform you, but the gem is worth nothing... putting it right on par with your pathetic life."

He brought the cane down against her head, causing her to black out into a dreamless slumber.

CHAPTER FIVE:
INNOCENCE

He looked at her, seeing the fear in her eyes and loving it.

Ian Char had always reveled in that fear, and found his home in it. Found comfort, even, the way most people find comfort in curling up next to a lover on a cold winter's night.

He had not known the touch of a lover in many years, but that was not to say he had not known the touch of a woman. Indeed, he had known the touch of many as their fists beat against his chest, begging for him to get off as he held their legs apart, before he eventually shot them, stabbed them, or otherwise made sure they would never tell a living soul what he had done.

This girl was older than the ones he usually picked, but she would do just fine. Most of the young ones were at the teen dance, and after everything that had happened in this town lately, they had taken to walking home in what could only be described as small packs.

He rolled up his sleeve with the hand that was not

holding a knife, revealing the red letter T tattooed on his upper arm. He smirked a little as the woman's eyes filled with even more fear, were that even possible. She recognized the symbol. That was always good. It meant that he wouldn't have to kill her, or deal with the body. It meant that she wouldn't tell a soul, anyway. The benefit of gang warfare.

"Please, don't," she begged, her groceries scattering the ground around her as she raised her arms to try and protect herself. "I won't tell anyone, I swear."

"I know you won't," Ian responded coldly, twirling the knife around in his hands. "You won't tell a single soul. You know that even if I went down, they'd come find you."

"Please," she whispered, as she realized her back was against the wall.

"Come on. Beg," he coaxed her, passing the blade playfully from hand to hand. "I love it when they beg."

The woman began to cry in heaping, helpless sobs.

"Why are you crying?" he said, sounding almost sympathetic. "It won't hurt..."

"Wrong," came a low, scratchy voice from behind him.

He turned, seeing the thing from his nightmares leaning against the far wall of the alleyway behind him, arms folded across its chest. Its skin was oily and thick. It was all black except for the eyes, which shone like twin red flames, burning with a passion for its work.

"It's going to hurt a lot, Ian."

"You!" Ian yelled, turning away from the woman and getting a better grip on his knife. "Why don't you go back where you came from? Things were great before you came!"

"And they say one person can't make a difference," the Womb barked, pushing off of the wall and into a relaxed fighting stance, fists at the ready.

Ian lunged forward with his blade, slashing at the beast. "Why can't you leave us alone?"

The Womb dodged, let the knife hit off the wall, then brought its knee up squarely into Ian's mid-section. "Why can't you stop raping women? Why does the world turn? Why is the sky blue? All these answers and more next time on Discovery Planet."

It drew back, releasing its claws with a sickening sound of bone ripping through flesh, and clawed Ian across the face. It reopened the wounds it had inflicted on the man weeks ago. The Womb leapt away from the bleeding mugger, then looked the woman up and down.

"Run!" it yelled, wondering why they always had to be told.

She took off, not bothering to pick up her groceries as she bolted down the block.

The Womb turned back toward Ian, only to find himself alone in the alley, catching a glimpse of the man as he took off into the night.

"Coward," he muttered as the blackness melted off him, revealing a thin layer of congealed blood covering his flesh. "You'd think this was the first time I whooped his ass."

He reached up and peeled the blood off of his body, then walked over to the dark corner where he'd left a white plastic shopping bag. He opened it, checked its contents, then started on his way again out of the alley and back toward the Peterson house.

They're getting brave again, Xander thought to himself, pulling his collar tight. *I thought the Tees had scattered after the last thrashing I gave them, but lately I've been seeing the signs again. People running away from shadows and not saying what. Rape victims that mysteriously drop charges against their attackers... and the cops. The cops aren't around this part of town as much, which means the cash flow from the Tees to the police has started again... with interest, I'd wager.*

I could figure out where they're hiding now... they're stupid enough to use that same warehouse off Laird, I'm betting. But maybe not. That leader of theirs... Roulette... he's not as dumb as he lets on. He's managed to get away with this crap for the last decade or more, so he must be doing something right.

At least the Tees are all that's on the streets, now that Genblade's in a coma and Derek's rotting in jail.

He turned into Julie's driveway, then skipped up the steps to her front door and opened it without knocking. It opened directly into the living room / kitchen / dining room / hallway, and Julie turned around in her spotted, torn couch to face him.

"What took you?" she asked innocently, glancing at the clock to make sure she wasn't being overzealous. "The store is, like, thirty seconds away."

"I ran into a friend on the way back," he smiled, leaning over from behind her and greeting her with a short kiss on the lips. "Had a chat with him for a minute."

"Anyone I know?"

"I hope not," he mumbled, plopping the bag down in front of the couch then hopping over it himself, landing next to her. The tightly coiled springs pushed into his rear.

"What?"

"Nothing."

Her eyes went directly for the bag, and she licked her lips a little. "Did you get it?"

"Get what?"

There was a moment then when they just looked at one another. He tried very hard to keep his face stalwart and stern, but a stupid grin was already starting to trickle along the sides of his mouth. She just looked at him, mouth partly open and eyes wide, waiting to see if he'd crack. Trying to figure him out.

"Don't tease," she decided finally, smiling contentedly as she turned toward the television. It was a thirteen-inch and sat on a box a few feet in front of the couch.

"I'm not. Was I supposed to get something?" His smirk was adamant now. He was only lying to himself by thinking that she didn't see through his flimsy ruse.

She sighed, letting him know that there was only so long that she'd put up with this game. "I said don't tease. I wouldn't mind if you were good at it, but you're a horrible liar."

"Is that so?"

She giggled. "'Tis so. 'Tis so indeed."

This time he really did have to ward off laughter. He felt his ribs ache with it, wanting to roll around on the floor at the joke that she hadn't even realized she'd made. Still, he kept it in, letting it pass with a quick cough aimed to one side, then returned her to his line of sight. "Well, I don't know that you're a good gauge for truth anyway."

"Yes. Right. Noted," she said impatiently, folding her arms in a cute, mock-pouting fashion. "Now, tell me that you got it."

He noted the change from *Did you get it* to *tell me you got it*, and decided to end the charade quickly before someone got hurt. Namely, him.

Rolling his eyes, he reached into the bag and pulled out a battered old VHS case.

"Yes," he said, defeated. "Yes, I got it."

She snatched it up and squealed with glee. She hugged the video cassette to her chest as if it were a small stuffed animal, leaning forward and giving him a quick peck on the lips.

The kiss took him aback and he fumbled a little on the chair, that stupid grin returning to his face. After a moment he shook it off, but his eyes still looked partially glazed over with pure, unadulterated schoolboy amazement at the feeling of her soft, silky lips.

"Hamina," he said, then shook his head to clear out the cobwebs she'd so easily placed there. "If that's what I get for the first one, I should have got the whole trilogy."

Julie smiled, getting up and bringing the tape over to the VCR. She bent over in an overtly sexualized manner and popped in the tape, somehow making that sexual as well.

He realized that she wasn't the only person completely comfortable with what was happening... he was, too. He remembered someone that he used to feel this comfortable with. Someone that he used to cuddle up on the couch with and watch cheesy movies, but even that was a far cry from this because she felt the same way now. She was reeling him in, and he felt no pain as the hook went into his mouth.

"I'm just glad you knew what I meant when I said 'The First One,'" she said slyly as she plopped down next to him, the springs digging at her. "When you took so long, I was starting to worry that you'd picked up Episode One."

"The Phantom Boredom?" he asked, cocking an eyebrow at her. "You think I'd waste five bucks on that piece of garbage?"

"I think you'd do just about anything I asked if you thought it might get you a little further," she smirked, her mouth moist and barely opening. Her eyes were half closed and fluttering over his body as she leaned in and gave him one slow, short kiss that rattled his entire frame. His every pore screamed for her to continue.

He smiled a true smile. A smile that he didn't even realize was there, it felt so normal. "I'm happy with where we are."

She gave him a quirked grin. "I know," she told him in a patronizing voice. "I was teasing. See? That's why I'm good at it."

He raised his arm. She snuggled into the spot he made for her, fitting as though she had been made for it, and he placed it comfortably around her, giving her one prolonged squeeze.

"Thank you," he said suddenly.

"For what?" she laughed, not taking her eyes off the screen as the decades old coming attractions came up, the tracking on the old tape jumping just enough to be annoying.

"For being a Warsie."

"A *what?*"

"A *Star Wars* fan. Apparently not enough that you know the terminology, though."

"Why is that such a big deal?"

"Do you have any idea how hard it is to find a girl that will request *Star Wars* for a movie?"

"As long as it's not Episode One," she chimed, shooting a finger dramatically into the air.

"As long as it's not Episode One," he agreed, nodding curtly.

"Jar Jar Binks must die."

"Too true."

Julie stopped for a moment. "Thank you."

"For what?" he asked, wondering if the conversation were about to repeat itself.

"For being the kind of guy you can watch movies with."

"There's another kind?"

She laughed at that, and it was just a little condescending. It was the laugh of someone with far more dating experience than he. "Yes. There are. There are guys that say they're going to watch the movie, put their arm around you, and then think you don't realize when they're trying to get your shirt off."

"I see," he coughed, not enjoying that mental picture in the least.

"No, you don't," she said, this time without the slightest hint of patronization. "That's what's great about you. You don't see how some people can be like that, and it's the best part of you. Not only are you not a jerk, but you can't get your head around how other guys can be jerks."

He huffed a little at that. "I've known my fair share of jerks."

"But none of them tried to get your clothes off."

He paused, a slight smile creeping onto his face. "There was one... but she turned out to be all right after all."

Julie blushed a little at that, burying her face in the crook of his arm. After a moment she poked her eyes up just enough to see if he was watching her. It was astonishingly cute. "I hoped you'd never mention that again."

"Abandon that hope," he chuckled, tickling her just a little with the arm that was wrapped around her.

She yelped at his surprise touch, jumping back up into her previous position.

He squeezed her again, then they both turned toward the screen in nearly perfect unison as the operatic instrumental started, and golden words began to scroll up onto the screen.

He held her close, and she him, and were as comfortable as they could be on a couch with springs poking out of it.

"I want to go home," Charles whined, stomping his foot, just to show that he knew what he was saying. Kids had a way of dramatizing simple things like that; it was part of their appeal. They could get away with so much that adults never could.

The whine cut through Malcolm's skull like a knife, slowly sawing at what he thought were the last remaining strands of his sanity. In fact, those strands had long since been sliced away. "Not yet. There's more candy. And you haven't even gotten the bread for your mother yet."

"I think I should go home." Tears were welling in the child's eyes now, his bottom lip quivering.

Malcolm sighed, not knowing what to do. The boy had wanted to come, had approached him. Surely they'd understand. What was he to do, send the child to that perverted obese man who looked like a country bumpkin inbred hick? No, he couldn't have that. The fat man would have abused the boy, taken advantage of him. Malcolm had fallen in love with the boy's golden locks. He would never hurt the child. Never.

Unless the boy wanted him to. Not hurt him, of course. He was not delusional. He knew that no child wished to be hurt. But if he was gentle... all kids these days knew about *it* (Malcolm blamed MTV). Charles, although sweet and innocent, was no different. He had wanted to follow Malcolm into the woods. Did he see what Malcolm had been doing there, hidden behind the shrub? Maybe the boy had wanted to be taken into the woods, his clothes hung on a tree.

He wouldn't hurt him. He'd be gentle, so gentle.

The boy might want it. Maybe that was why he was crying. Crying because he didn't feel he was beautiful, thought Malcolm. Maybe he did not like the golden curls his mother had tried to rid him of.

Suddenly, Malcolm had the image of holding the boy's head down where Malcolm's hand had been earlier, and running his fingers through those golden curls.

Don't do that, Malcolm.

"Shh," he hissed quietly, not wanting to alert the child

to the others about. They might try to hurt him, and Malcolm never would.

"I want -"

"I was just talking to your mommy," he said suddenly. He said the words before he even really thought them. "She said it was dark out and that you shouldn't walk home. Isn't that what Mommy tells you?"

Slowly, Charles nodded.

"Your Mommy said you should stay here tonight. She'll see you tomorrow. If you want?"

Again, the child slowly nodded.

See, thought Malcolm, I knew he wanted to.

Don't do that, Malcolm.

"Shh."

CHAPTER SIX:
SOUND COUNCIL

Dr. Warren O'Toole walked through the hallway of Coral Beach High, waving to students who never waved back as he passed. Over the past month they'd come to regard him as the boogeyman, and the children that were regulars in his office had taken on a dubious reputation of their own. Not one to be outdone, when he caught the teens mocking his patients, he'd use the authority that Principal Shnieder had reluctantly given him to bring the bullies into therapy, hoping that eventually he and his patients would be viewed as just as normal as anyone else.

This day, on the other hand, his courteous waves were just a charade. In fact, he was having what could only be described as the world's worst day.

He'd picked out his favorite blue dress shirt to wear to work that morning. He was only inside the front doors of the building for thirty seconds when an overly energetic seventh grader had shoved past him, making him spill hot coffee all over himself.

That thought in mind, he reminded himself again to

call the boy's parents and suggest Ritalin to them.

When he made it to his office his tie had gotten caught in his door as he closed it, ripping down the middle. Now only the top half of Mickey Mouse's head was visible, making him feel like an Indian to Mickey's cowboy from one of those old forties Disney flicks gone horribly wrong.

Then, he stubbed his toe on the edge of his desk. Normally not an overly painful experience, but he happened to have a hangnail on that exact appendage. The pinky, of all things.

Around this point in time, he was beginning to feel like an unwitting victim on *Candid Camera*.

Then, Shnieder came into his office, looking more weaselish than ever, and informed him that a young girl in grade eight named Tracy Hoder was pregnant, and she did not know who the father was, so she was being sent to him on a weekly basis to help deal with her oncoming emotional difficulties.

So he was already having a bad day when his two o'clock appointment didn't show up.

If this had been any other child, he would have written a detention slip and relished in the hour of relaxation, but, of course, this student was Alexander Drew.

O'Toole called Xander's teachers. Yes, he was in school today. No, none of them knew where he was. They thought he was supposed to be with him.

He wondered if Shnieder would eventually crack and allow him to start writing detention slips for teachers. He ran his hands through his thick black hair, taking off his tinted glasses every five minutes to make sure that they weren't dirty, and waved politely to people as he scoured the halls looking for his lost patient.

He poked his head into the lunch room, getting an annoyed glance from a small group of senior students sitting in a semi-circle and pretending to study. He raised a hand in apology, then quickly backed out of the room again.

Where is that kid? he growled inwardly, trying to keep himself calm as he felt his blood pressure rise past normally acceptable levels. *Maybe I should bring Xander in to meet my physician,* he thought whimsically as he darted in and out of classrooms. He even poked his head in through the men's room, finding nothing but more annoyed teenagers. *Maybe he'd up his Xanax dosage...*

He passed by the locker room, at first seeing nothing but a row of sickly green lockers. As he was ducking out again, a slight motion caught his eye. He turned back swiftly, seeing it for what it was: the female form pressed against the male form. Teenagers making out in the locker room.

With a wry smile, he turned away and continued on his search.

He was ten steps down the hall before he stopped.

Turning on his heel, he stomped back toward the locker room, fists clenched into tight little balls of repressed rage. He came back to the entrance of the room and stood in the doorway, getting another good look at what he saw there.

After he was done his double-take, his blood pressure was higher than it ever had been in the months since Xander had come under his care.

"Xander!" he yelled, and Julie leapt from his arms, no longer pinning him against the lockers in unbridled passion.

"Mr. O'Toole..." she stammered, fighting to catch her breath after the fright and the exhilaration of the kiss. "I mean, ah, Dr. Warren... Mr. Warren..."

"Dr. O'Toole?" he volunteered, through clenched teeth.

"That's it," she agreed, nodding and trying to hide her smile through pursed lips. "You know, Alexander and I were just talking about you."

Xander just stood with his back against the wall, looking totally dumbfounded. He still wore that silly smile he'd had on last night, the one all teenage boys get after kissing beautiful young girls.

"Really?" O'Toole ventured sarcastically, giving Xander a look.

"Oh, yeah," she assured him, trying her best to appear innocent. "I was just giving him a kiss for luck. He really wanted to impress you with his, um, thoughts on what he's been... feeling lately."

"Has he been not been feeling well?" Warren asked, his voice laced think with mock concern.

Julie could not suppress her smile any longer. "No, actually. He feels quite well."

"I'm sure," he barked, then turned to Xander. "And what about you? Where's your usual dry wit when I'm finally in the mood for it, hmm? Cat got your tongue?"

Xander shook his head without opening his mouth, looking rather sheepish.

"What then?"

He reached into his mouth, pulling out a small, metallic loop.

"Earring," he said simply, with an awful smile pasted across his lips.

Julie's hand immediately went up to her right ear in shock. She grabbed the jewelry back and started to place it back inside her lobe. "About that, Dr. O'Toole... it's a good luck thing... my family's French you see, and - "

"Really?" O'Toole interrupted, taking one menacing step forward. "My family's French, and I never heard of that particular tradition before. What part of France did you say your family was from?"

"Well," she stammered, her tongue feeling like it was doing cartoon loops inside her mouth. "You see - "

"Go to Shnieder's office, young lady," he ordered, waving to dismiss her.

"Yes, sir," she said, skittering away as quickly as she could.

He took a step toward Xander, shaking his head in dismay. "We had an appointment, young man."

Xander said nothing, but met the older man's gaze head on. Now that Julie was gone they'd both taken off all masks of civility. They'd been playing this same game for far too long to bother with it, and found it more efficient to skip the pleasantries.

"You never learn, do you?" he asked, throwing his hands into the air. "I try, and I try to get it through that thick skull of yours that I'm trying to help you, but you don't listen. You don't get it. You never will, either. You'd rather just run around acting stupid, shirking your responsibilities this way and that to go off with some girl."

"Watch it," Xander said bluntly, curling his upper lip.

O'Toole froze for a moment, then slowly lowered his

hands and stood up perfectly straight. The only indication of his altering mood was that his eyebrows had sunken down below his glasses to become hidden. "Excuse me?" he said finally, after giving Xander a moment to alter his confrontational tone.

"You heard me," Xander said again, cocking his head at the counselor. "Don't pretend to know about my responsibilities, or what I feel responsible for. You have no sweet clue..."

"Okay, listen," Warren started, putting his hands in the air.

"No," Xander barked, shaking his head. "You listen. I've been listening to you yammer on and on for two months now, and I gotta say, I'm bloody sick of it. A few weeks ago, a little girl was kidnapped. I was out every night until at least four in the morning, searching for her through mud and grime and brush -"

"All right, I -"

"When I'm done, you can speak," Xander demanded, shutting the older man up quickly. "I found that little girl's arm. Her *arm*. It was buried under a foot of soil. You know who else was out searching? Gang members. Jerks, criminals, and psychos. You know who wasn't?" He paused, giving the words a second to sink in. "You, Warren. You didn't step foot outside your office, and now you're consoling the people close to her as if you have any idea what you're talking about, and then you're surprised when it doesn't work."

"I only meant that -"

"I'm not finished. If I want to blow off one of your insipid lectures to relax a little, to pretend for five seconds that I have a normal life, I will. So, tell you what, when the next kid goes missing? You look," he snarled, looking the man up and down with an expression of utter disgust. "'Cause I'm on vacation."

Xander moved to brush past O'Toole, feeling more than a little proud of himself.

"And what about Julie?" O'Toole asked, turning again toward Xander, the fluorescent lights gleaming sinisterly off his glasses.

"Fuck you," Xander shot, continuing to walk past.

O'Toole lunged out, pressing his palms against Xander's shoulders and shoving him.

Hard.

Xander went back against the lockers, denting them upon impact, to the sound of grinding metal as the hinges ached and strained.

"Hey!" Xander screamed, rubbing his shoulder.

"You're right, Drew!" O'Toole shouted, pointing a finger in Xander's face, all but pinning him against the lockers as the older man's face turned livid with anger. "Maybe you do deserve a normal life. But that girl does, too. She's been through more than you, even if you're too self-absorbed to admit it. She's been raped. She's been beaten. Worst of all, she's been denied... the latter of which by you. Now that you need a break, you decide you like her? Huh? What happens when you want to go back to the way things were? Are you going to just throw her aside again?"

"Maybe I don't want to go back to the way I was. Maybe I'm sick of digging up arms."

"If we had a choice about what fate wanted for us, I

wouldn't be in a locker room that smells like shit lecturing a child whose father should have given him a couple hard smacks. But we don't have a choice, and eventually, you're either going to hurt her, or they'll be digging up her arm in a field."

Xander paused, shaking his head. "I'm not going to let Julie get hurt."

"Like Sara?" O'Toole snapped, again shoving Xander's back against the locker.

Xander's eyes bulged with anger, his heart sending boiling blood throughout his veins. Then, without warning, the true-womb organ began to twitch. Slowly coming to life, it started pumping blackness throughout his body, filling it until it felt ready to burst, taking over.

When he realized what was happening he stopped, the anger fading from his face and falling into desperation. O'Toole, although he couldn't possibly know it, was right. Emotion was a major trigger of the Black Womb. If he almost transformed out of anger... there was nothing saying that strong emotions caused by Julie couldn't do it too. Slowly, he nodded.

"You're right," he agreed, forcing his voice to be its normal, human self, despite the growing frog in his throat.

O'Toole relaxed a little then, motioning back toward the door. "It's time for another hypnosis session," he said, smirking. "And if kissing a girl is the worst thing you do at age fifteen, believe me, I shouldn't be saying anything to you."

Xander forced a smile as he followed the man back to his office.

ʎ꙰ʎ

*Warren O'Toole has an attitude problem. I think maybe he
didn't get enough attention as a child. Or maybe too much...
don't ask me, I don't know anything about this kind of stuff.
But, like, neither does he.*

Mandy Peterson sat in class, her Geography textbook
stood up in front of her on her desk, hiding the fact that
she was writing in her notebook instead of paying attention to whatever the teacher was rambling about.

The desk she was sitting at was riddled with graffiti
pledging allegiance to popular musicians, sexual commentary, and information for those who wanted to know
who was easy in the class. She had taken care to erase her
name from the list every day, and every day it appeared
again, like some phantom was floating around late at night
with a pencil, intent on making her life miserable.

*He's, like, totally a herb. A troll. Beyond help of any kind.
He thinks that he's doing us a favor by making us dredge up all
these things from our pasts, confronting old ghosts and all that
psycho-babble bull. Really all he's doing is reminding us how
horrible everything is, not letting us forget.*

Like Xander.

*He's totally the school sweetheart. No doubt about it, that's
why he's the outcast. Everyone knows they'll never be what
comes so easily to him, no matter how hard they try. The sad
thing about him (and the reason that I'll never understand what
Julie sees in him), is that nobody will ever convince him that
he's there.*

*He wants to be some kind of saint. I think it's because of
Mike, because of everything Mike does to make this town a bet-*

ter place, to help people. It's jealousy. But he's there. He's right up there with Mike and the rest of the big-time superheroes, but he'll never understand that. No matter how many times you tell him he's there, he'll look at you and say, like: "You're wrong. I'm almost there, I just need this one last step."

In his mind, he'll always need to go that one step farther.

That's why these sessions with O'Toole are bad for all of us. It makes us think that we have to accomplish something to be at peace, that we have to face these demons to be free. Really, to be at peace and be free... just, like, do it. Say: I am at peace, I am free; and then believe it. There. Done. Mission accomplished. No psycho-babble or twenty minute hypnosis needed. Just do it, like the sign says.

Mike's a different story. He's a guy who should be saying that he's just one step away. Him and Cathy have been terminal for a while... last night at the dance only proved that. I felt the way he held me, the way we laughed at stuff we never would have even talked about with other people. But he thinks everything's okay, peachy. He doesn't even realize how fast it'll all come crashing down.

And I don't really want to be around when it does.

Because the only thing worse than Cathy's cold stares is the look in Mike's eyes when he's really mad. He doesn't even look like himself anymore. He changes, I don't know how or why, but he becomes someone different when he's mad.

He becomes the Black Womb.

He became it to save me from the Tee's last month, first when I moved here from Coral Cove. They were going to kill me, and he came in. Xander says it wasn't him, but I know it was. Is Xander lying... or does he not know what Mike is?

I hope he does, because there's only one thing Mike looks at *worse than he did the Tee's, and that's guys that try for Cathy.*

And there's only one person Xander looks at more than Julie, and that's Cathy.

No matter what way the bread gets sliced, Xander's the one who's going to be bleeding.

Xander Drew.

Mike Harris.

Tommy Irons.

"Keith Richardson?" Mr. Miles called out across the room. A hand was raised unceremoniously by Keith, letting the old Boston teacher know that he was present.

The names were scrawled on Cathy's desk in dark red ink, splotching involuntarily at times, turning it just a little darker and making it look like blood.

"Pamela Walsh?"

There were more names there, though. People that she had never seen, and yet she had come to know very well in the past month.

Cora.

Gwen.

Alexandra.

Amora.

Sarah.

Cora was after the town, Coral Beach. Although it had done so much to her, she still loved it more than any other place on earth. It was where her family had their first home. It was where she'd met her childhood friends and where most of them were buried, each gravestone like a place in her past to be visited periodically.

Gwen was after a character on Xander's favorite show growing up. She'd never watched it herself, but had heard it in that background a few times and couldn't help noticing it. The name, for some reason, had stuck in her mind as a symbol of beauty and grace.

Alexandra was an obvious spin on Xander's name, the recipient of it maybe even being referred to lovingly as Xandra (pronounced 'Sandra'). She had thought of it once while Xander was recounting the way he got his name. He had told her that the nuns at his orphanage had named the children for saints, like Saint Alexander. Since there was an Alexander and an Alex already, he got saddled with the name Xander. She thought about a fourth combination from the name, and its feminine version came to mind after only a few moments of thought.

"Leonard Kirby? Leona - ah, there."

Amora. In Norse mythology, which her father had always had an obscure fixation with, Amora was the goddess of love. It seemed a very fitting name, both in reference to her father's hobby and the emotion itself. She pictured the recipient being eyed by boys, whose name they loved to roll off their tongues.

And Sarah.

That one was too obvious, named for her dead best friend Sara Johnson. But she'd never liked the idea of naming directly. She didn't want this new person to be 'Sara the second,' so a letter 'h' was added for clarity.

There was another list of names too, albeit not quite as long.

Darrell.

Duncan.

Mike.

Darrell had been her grandfather's name, and was also her father's middle name. It was important, she thought, to keep some of that alive, especially since it was perhaps the one good reason that her father had wanted to have boys.

Duncan, after her Uncle Duncan Ross (on her mother's side), who had died of cancer two years previous.

Mike... Mike, after the father.

The names were those never chosen, never needing to be chosen, for the child she never had. The child robbed of her. Taken by a monster as well as monstrous events. It had been inside of her. She had felt it as much as she had felt the father's presence within her for the all too brief time he had been there. And now it was gone. But unlike most mothers, who got to hold their babies when their time carrying it was through, Cathy only got empty arms and a gaping hole where her heart had been to match.

It was like when her child had left her in tiny seeps of blood, it had grabbed onto her insides to try and stay, accidentally taking something with it. Now there was just that void, and no knowledge of how to fill it.

The names could be matched, of course. Middle names and all.

There was Sarah Alexandra Harris... that seemed right, to put those two together in a way their counterparts never got a chance to be. Poetic, almost.

Darrel Michael, which just sounded right.

However, she never considered Cora Amora. That just seemed like it would be a lapse in good judgement, or the mark of a truly cruel parent.

"Calla McFadden?"

Not far down from that list was another, far longer than any of the others.

It was a list of her dead.

Jamie Dawkins.

Liz Tyler.

Kerri Walker.

Sara Johnson.

Roxanne Carpenter.

- -

Her pen tapped nervously upon the space at the end. The emptiness from it seemed to glare up at her, ordering her to put something there. There was another name to be added to the list, it needed to be there to commemorate such a tragic loss of life. But the person she wanted to remember never had a name, just a short list of potential names.

So the space remained.

And with nothing to hang onto, no graves, no scribbling on a beaten old desk, no spot in her memory to visit whenever she needed to, the gap just floated there in the back of her mind at all times, calling out for attention like a child in the mid-summer night.

"Cathy Kennessy?" Miles called, pointing a pen across the room slowly as he tried to find her.

Cathy's head popped up, shaking her from her trance.

"Here," she said sheepishly, then lowered her head and entered that hollow area inside herself again. The next thing to bring her out was the bell to end class.

CHAPTER SEVEN
SPYDER SPYDER

Coral Beach Penitentiary.

Home to some of the most vile and disgusting criminal minds ever to come out of New England, its extremely underfunded budget had recently come under scrutiny by the state legal commission.

Sexual sadists shared the same walls as mass murderers, both from the town and the surrounding areas. It had been transformed from a simple court holding facility to a full-fledged prison in the early seventies, when an upsurge of criminal activity had plagued the township. It currently housed seventy-three inmates.

One of them was sleeping so deep that the compounds modest medical staff has predicted that he would never wake up inside his lifetime.

That inmate was named Adam Genblade.

Genblade had lived his life within concrete walls, first at the Engen facility where he was born, and now at the prison. He had only been outside such walls twice, both within the last five months.

He will die here, spilling out the remains of his bowels and bladder into the bedpan that now rests partially beneath him, one final insult to the town that he reaped so much chaos on.

An oxygen mask covered the lower half of his face, a mechanical ventilator barely a foot away pumping air into his massive lungs for him. Intravenous needles punctured his cast arms in multiple places, providing him the drugs and nutrients he needed to stay alive and to heal his body, if not his mind. A chart at the foot of the bed kept logs of his brainwave activity, of which there was none. Scabs and scars littered his bare chest, memories of battles both recent and historic. His eye was swollen beyond comprehension.

Although it was difficult to see, several of his filed-down back teeth had been broken and now lay somewhere inside his colon. Soon he would pass them, leaving a nasty surprise of blood and enamel in his bedpan for the nurse.

The door to his room opened and two nurses entered, one wheeling in a cart with a fresh IV bag for the patient. The other went to the computer readout that had monitored his heart rate, brain activity and respiratory pace for the last twenty-four hours.

"Let's see what you're trying to tell us today, Mr. Genblade," Nurse Reilly said, making a few quick clicks on the keyboard to bring up that day's report. "Anything interesting going on in that head of yours?"

The other nurse, an African American woman named Nurse Porter, unhooked the old, shrunken IV bag and prepared a full one.

"While you're over there," Reilly chimed, glancing over her shoulder as she continued to type. "Don't forget to check the pan for surprises."

Porter stopped what she was doing, put her hands on her hips, and glowered. "I checked it yesterday. Cleaned it, too."

"I'm pretty sure I did it yesterday."

"I'm sure you didn't."

"Just do your job."

"I think we need a calendar for this. To keep track."

"Stop whining. Did you catch Leno last night?"

"Naw. He sucks, I'd rather watch Kimmel, and that's saying -"

Nurse Porter stopped what she was doing, jumping just a little as her heart began to flutter. Reilly turned as well, not taking her eyes off the object of her fright. There, standing in the doorway, was a tall man dressed completely in robes, holding what looked to be an elaborate cane.

His face and chin were slender and free of blemishes, making him look like he could have been a member of a boy band in his younger years. His hair, which came down around either one of his nearly clear blue eyes in great streaks, was coal black and shone under the fluorescent lights. His lips were small and tight, and he wore a lace bandana across his head with a gemstone in its center, just up from being directly between his eyes. A second stone was on another piece of cloth, wrapped around his right hand so that the stone was flat against his palm.

He regarded the nurses with very little fascination.

"Who are you?" Reilly finally got up the nerve to ask.

"I am Sebastian LeGaea," he said with such magnitude, importance, and imperialism that he made it seem like he was saying 'I am Jesus Christ.' He had a thick Scandinavian accent.

"You're really not allowed in here. This is a secure facility," Reilly informed him, crossing her arms.

He let out a very dry laugh, which to anyone else would have sounded fake, but on him was just right. A regal laugh, of someone being amused by the actions of those beneath him. "Secure. Yes, very. I walked in through the front entrance while the man out front was reading a vulgar monthly publication featuring anorexic, nude teenage girls. The definition of security has changed, hasn't it?"

Reilly looked stunned, gave Porter a look, then turned back to LeGaea. "I guess... so? Anyway, I don't care how you got in, I'm telling you that you have to leave. This is a very dangerous man."

Again, laughter. LeGaea surveyed Genblade, giving him a brief once over. "Again, I feel the definition of the word has changed since I first used it."

"The patient is not to be seen," she spat in finalization, using words that she was sure he could not mock or bounce back at her in his pretty-boy accent again. "Leave."

LeGaea stood a moment, watching her with an expressionless face, the small twitches near the corners of his tiny lips probably the closest he ever came to a smile. "I'm afraid I cannot do that yet. You see, this man has chanced upon something I need. A part of the Tri-Ok'Force. Useless on its own, but with the other two... not so useless."

"Well," Porter said, finally finding her voice. "Like the

song says: two out of three ain't bad. Scram."

LeGaea, again without the slightest hint of change to his face, regarded the woman as if he had only just realized she was there. "If only that were true. However, in this instance, it is not so. Please discontinue swaying me from my path, or I will strike one of you in the left temple and the other in the jaw, rendering you both unconsciousness, neither of which I wish to do unless otherwise compelled."

"That's it," Reilly growled, moving quickly to the wall and reaching for the direct line to security. "I've had just about enough of you, Prince Charles."

As she reached out to pick up the phone, LeGaea took one menacing step toward her. His robes billowed behind him, flapping like flags in the wind, the symbols on its lining seeming to move of their own accord.

Reilly reached up to block her face from his attack, her mouth agape, but was too late. He bent his elbow high and shot it forward, cracking her in the left temple with it. As she fell in a heap to the ground, Porter's eyes went wide and she opened her mouth to scream.

LeGaea turned, whipped his cane forward and threw it. It spun once before meeting its target, the grip connecting with Porter's jaw and shattering it, sending teeth scattering to the floor. The cane bounced back toward him, and he bent over and picked it up, its simple black wooden handle again resting in his palm.

Porter hit the floor, and did not get back up.

"I told you, you did not listen. That is the problem with American women," he admonished, stepping over Reilly's body, his heels clicking against the tile floor. He turned to look at Genblade, as helpless as a newborn kitten in a sack at the pier. There were even still open wounds from biopsies all over his once magnificent, but now broken, form. Sebastian balked, leaning over and spitting ceremoniously, the saliva hitting Genblade on the forehead. He then continued to a locked steel cage on the other side of the room, guarded by a computerized keypad. Casually, he raised the end of his cane to it and shocked it with electric blue energy. He was temporarily bathed in sinister shadows, then reached out and simply opened the door.

He walked down the long hallway, past row upon row of lockers and safes, along with bags of contraband and cocaine he could smell from the hallway. Near the end was a locker on which a placard read: Genblade, A.

He opened the unlocked cabinet, revealing two identical items inside: the Spider-Swords. Gifts from the Engen higher-ups to their greatest weapon, Eve Spider, Adam's dead wife. After her murder, they had become Genblade's. Now, it seemed, they belonged to LeGaea.

He carefully lay his cane against the lockers, and slowly began to unwrap the cloth around his hand, which held the gem of Aberdean in place. When it came loose, he held it in the palm of his hand, bringing it to touch the gem on his forehead. With his free hand, he reached out and touched one of the swords, then the other. He picked up the second, feeling its weight in his hand. He twirled it once, admiring the way it moved. His mouth again twitched in what might have passed for a grin as he reached out and removed the ruby that made up the glimmering torso of the spider decorating the handle of the blade, holding it to his head as well.

A big, broad smile spread across his lips. He took the gems down, then wrapped the Spider-Gem in cloth around his left hand, and Aberdean around his right.

The smile faded confidently from his lips until he was back to his formal postulate. He picked up his cane and walked toward the exit, his robes billowing behind him.

CHAPTER EIGHT:
IGNORANCE

Xander awoke with a start, and for a moment he just laid there with his eyes roaming back and forth across the stucco ceiling, unsure of his surroundings. He felt sweaty and uncomfortable in his clothes, like they were a little too loose on him. His mouth was dry and the bright fluorescent lights shining down on him stung his pupils.

For a brief moment, he thought he was back at Engen.

Then, a familiar voice snapped him away from that thought.

"Well, that was a good session," Dr. O'Toole said cheerily, tucking his pocket watch into his front pocket, then used a handkerchief to quickly wipe his hands. The watch glimmered for a moment before disappearing into the tall man's pocket completely.

Xander sat up slowly. His back ached horribly and his head was pounding to the beat of a Jamaican drum. He got a head rush as he moved, multicoloured spots splotching his vision, each one representing a different kind of pain.

"Ugh."

"Something the matter?" O'Toole asked, with something very close to actual concern, as he turned his back to Xander and poured himself a cup of coffee from the little One-Cup on his bookshelf.

"My head hurts a little," he answered, rubbing the bridge of his nose.

"You probably just sat up too fast. Coffee?"

Xander raised an eyebrow to the man, glancing at the coffee maker. "Thanks, but I'll pass."

"Also, your smoking could be causing your headache," O'Toole offered, giving him the *you should quit* look, but not actually saying it. "It's probably nothing, but I could prescribe some pain killers if it keeps up..."

"No," Xander replied, waving his hand in dismissal. "No, I'll be fine."

Warren shrugged, then nodded. "All right, then. Would you like to talk about your therapy now?"

Xander shot him a look. "No, but by order of Shnieder, I have to, don't I?"

"Glad to see you're so cooperative," the counselor said sarcastically. "I'll keep it quick, though. I'm sure you want to go see Miss Peterson."

Xander got a little quiet then. "Yeah, I guess... yes, let's make it quick."

"Your progress is coming along nicely. It seems like every time you go under, you have less and less stress than the previous times. It's really quite wonderful. Have you been feeling the effects yourself?"

Xander paused, letting the question bounce around in his head for a moment. "A little, I guess. I can't say I have any less stress, but it has been easier to relax lately."

O'Toole nodded, smiling. "That's because the stress these sessions help relieve you of was putting pressure on your subconscious. You won't wake up after being hypnotized and all your homework be done, your girl having forgiven you, and to your parents having raised your allowance."

"If it were like that, I wouldn't be so reluctant." Xander pointed out with a whimsical smile.

"Hah. Yes. But seriously, what the work we do here means is that when the homework is done, the girlfriend is happy, and the money is spent... it'll be easier for you to wind down because there aren't a thousand things eating at you that you aren't even aware of."

Xander frowned. "That makes sense, I guess."

"So, can I expect you to be on time next week?"

Xander smiled devilishly. "Depends on whether or not I get distracted. Either way, you know where to find me."

꘎

Xander closed the door to O'Toole's office, a smile on his face that he could not suppress. Even his sessions with O'Toole were getting easier. The guy seemed to actually be developing a personality, which was a bonus. Life as the Womb was getting easier to handle; he wasn't transforming at night when he went to sleep half as often as he did just a few months ago... he wasn't even transforming a third as much as he had the first few weeks he got his powers. Even when he did transform, it was much easier to control the Womb now, no aqua-eyes in sight.

Even though things between Mike and Cathy were rough, things between he and each of them separately hadn't been better in months. Mandy was being a real cutie lately, and things with Julie were making his life happier than ever. All and all, things were going great.

He turned the corner around the office, and saw Mike leaning against the wall waiting for him. Mike frowned, looking up from the floor.

"We've gotta talk," he said hoarsely, his throat raw from fresh tears.

⋏⋎⋏

Xander stared at the tiled floor before him, his own vision steadily becoming blurry and wet. His lower lip quivered violently, and he could not bear to lift his head.

"How old is he?" he managed finally, turning to Mike. His friend was already crying again, rubbing the knuckles, which were sore from punching the walls of the school while he had waited for Xander.

"About nine, give or take. I could call a few and ask, but..."

"It's not important," Xander finished, placing a hand on his friend's shoulder. "I know."

The cafeteria they sat in was vacant, not even the workers were there. The echoes all around them were steady and haunting, like voices crying out at them from just beyond their sight.

"Those neighborhood watch people that have been popping up since... well, since the last time this happened? They're out in full force now. I don't think there's any way we'll even be able to make it onto the street without bumping into them."

"So using the Womb to track him isn't an option," Xander sighed, leaning back in his chair as his brain began to ache from trying to work out the situation.

There was a long pause, then Mike finally looked up, his voice accusatory. "Is it possible that this is Zakron?"

Xander's eyes went wide as he considered that, reliving his last few moments with the twisted fun-house-mirror version of himself.

"No," he answered finally, shaking his head. "No, this isn't him."

Mike threw his head back, breathing a sigh of relief. "Thank you, God." When his head came back around, his expression was a form of joy, but more than anything, a sickening guilt. "I know that shouldn't make a difference. There's still a kid out there... but it just makes it-"

"I know," Xander nodded, raising his hand to allow his friend to stop explaining himself. "You have every right to feel that way. I do too. But if we're dealing with a human here, then the chances are even slimmer that this kid is going to be found in one piece."

"How's that?"

"At least with Zakron we could predict him. He was an animal, he followed instinct. Whoever this is is a *person*, and that's a way sicker animal. If the police or the neighborhood watch handle this the wrong way, this kid is going to wish he was Kerri Walker."

"All right, all right," Mike said, waving his arms for his friend to stop talking. "What can we do?"

"With underprivileged soccer-moms roaming the streets? Not so much. You know I hate to say this... but I think we might just have to call it a night on this one, at least for now."

"What?" he said, jumping out of his chair.

"*For now*," Xander reiterated, easing his friend to calm down. "We can't do anything. With Zakron, if he caught me behind him one night, he wouldn't even realize I was looking for the kid. If this creep even feels you or the Black Womb looking down his back, he'll murder that kid and use his blood to paint a giant 'Helter Skelter' across Coral Beach, you catch my drift?"

Mike shook his head in defiance, his eyes now glued to the floor. "So, what are we going to do?"

The bell rang, startling Mike, but Xander just sat in the same position.

"We're going to go outside. I'm going to smoke, you're going to ask for a draw to calm your nerves, and we're going to eat our lunches with the girls because it's been a long day."

Mike sighed and started walking toward the door, Xander tagging along close behind. "You don't have to come. You should, but you don't have to. But you can't stop me from looking for that kid."

Xander frowned, squeezing his friend's shoulder. "You keep believing that, man."

᚛⋎᚜

Macy Walker looked out her back window, staring at one spot in the ground: a fading patch of green grass, dulling in the longing fall months, until soon there would be hardly any colour left to it at all.

That was the last place where she had seen her daughter, playing with the leaves, her long, curly black hair streaming behind her. She was wearing a dark blue dress and sparkly red shoes that looked like they had come right out of the Wizard of Oz, which she had watched nearly seventy times, always with a new sense of wonder in those big, amazing brown eyes of hers.

Macy had sent her out to play because Kerri was always a bug while she was doing the dishes, pulling on her pant leg, wanting to help, wanting to get up in her arms, wanting to play... just wanting attention, really. What did a child that age care if the dishes got done or not? She'd probably just as soon buy paper plates to eat off all the time, then throw them away.

She had seen her daughter once since then, but at the same time, had not seen her.

She had gone with the child's father, George, to identify their baby's body at the city morgue. Her arm was missing, and the rest of her tiny body was beaten and ravaged almost beyond recognition. She remembered shaking her head yes when they asked her: "Is this your daughter?"

But it wasn't.

Her daughter didn't look like that. Her daughter had eyes that glistened in the moonlight while she read bedtime stories about Lions and Witches living within a magical wardrobe. No, that hadn't been her daughter. Somewhere, she was sure, her daughter was still playing in the grass, chasing leaves and following butterflies all around. Somewhere, in a world far better than this one, she was safe. Macy was sure of it.

She turned briefly from the scummy dishes and the kitchen window, looking at the rest of the small house that seemed entirely too big now that it was just she and her husband living in it.

The living room was a jumble of papers and old editions of the Beach News Daily, along with posters that the neighborhood watch people had given them. Each was a large piece of bristle-board with Kerri's face printed on it, followed by two bolded words: Never Again.

Never Again.

Who were they to make such a ridiculous promise?

Her child's killer had never even been caught. He was still out there somewhere, smirking about what he'd done to her little body, how he'd crushed her tiny soul beneath the weight of him. She could picture him. Sometimes, she thought that maybe she saw him in the supermarket, or in the mall. Those people that gave her polite nods of respect and fake smiles... there was always someone whose smile did not seem all that fake.

And now there was another child missing. A young boy, not much older than Kerri had been. How long would it be before some punk teenager found his arm in a ditch? Next there would be signs up all around town with his face on it saying Never Again and everyone would forget about Kerri. Everyone except for her.

Never Again? It had been a little over a week, and already people had found something new. How could they stop this from happening to another child when the demon that did it was still out there?

Over at the Town Office, they'd started up a memorial: a giant wall for all the people that had been murdered in this town. She and George had wanted Kerri's name up there... but they wouldn't allow it. Kerri had not been born in Coral Beach, George had moved them back to his hometown a little after she turned one. By that stupid bureaucracy, they would have to pay a fee of two hundred and fifty dollars to get her name on the wall.

George was down at the Daily arguing the point now, but it would make no difference. The people at the town office were adamant. George had been laid off a few months ago, and they could not afford the money.

So with nothing to remember her little girl by, not even a body that looked like her, Macy Walker took her only comfort in the words Never Again... words that she not only disbelieved, but had already been proven wrong.

᛭

Xander took a puff of his cigarette, tapping it twice and watching the ashes fall toward the butt-littered ground around the side of the school. Just a few yards down was the new patch of temporary building, there because of the Zakron's attack when it came to search out the Black Womb. That part of the building would be fully rebuilt in the spring, but right now it had just been closed off for repairs until after the snow melted.

He kept one eye trained on Julie, who was sitting across the fenced-in field alongside the school. She was sitting on the picnic table that faced the south entrance, as she usually did, eating her bag of chips and sipping on the Pepsi she'd gotten from the cafeteria. She glanced over at him for a moment, throwing him a friendly, nearly seductive wave as she turned back to Cathy and Mandy, talking about some unknown subject that girls were wont to do when men could not hear.

"God, that girl is beautiful," he said wistfully, taking another long drag.

"Aren't you supposed to be quitting that?" Mike scoffed, waving the smoke Xander was exhaling away from his face, although the steady breeze seemed determined to keep it there.

"Naw, I tend to like it. I don't need to eat now, so I need something stupid to spend all of my money on. This works. Plus, healing factor. Don't have to worry about cancer."

"Your teeth could still turn yellow."

"Crest whitening, man. Duh."

"Fine. Do what you want. See if I care."

There was a moment then, as Xander turned and waved at Julie again.

"All right," Xander said, finally. "Cathy's not looking."

"Finally!" Mike frowned, throwing an accusatory glare at his friend as he took the smoke. He took quick, steady puffs and inhaled them back as fast as he could while Xander kept an eye on their respective girlfriends.

"So, what's the deal with Mandy?" Xander asked.

"What deal? There's no deal." Mike said quickly, between hauls.

Xander turned, smirking at his friend. "He protesteth too much, methinks?"

"Shut up."

He chuckled, taking the smoke back from Mike to savor the last few draws. "I only meant that even though she hasn't told us about what happened to her, we know. I think it's cool that you're not freaking out about her asking you to dance and stuff, just be sure you know the line between being nice and leading her on."

"Thanks," Mike nodded appreciatively, smirking. "And I do know the line. Dancing and talking is the line, the occasional hug when there's nobody around to give it. That's all this is going to be."

"That's great, man." Xander said, impressed with his friend's turnaround. "Now, I think we gotta head back over to the girls."

∧⟨⟩∧

Xander walked right up to Julie and gave her a kiss, a smile spreading across his lips as he pulled away. She wrapped her hand around the back of his neck and pulled him back in gently for a longer one, not satisfied with what he'd provided.

"We still on for tonight?" he asked her between smacks.

She did not even bother to part her lips to respond, merely shook her head in agreement.

Mandy rolled her eyes. "P.D.A at twelve o'clock," she groaned, turning to Mike. "Totally unnecessary."

"Yeah," Mike agreed, tapping Xander on the back for him to stop.

They did not.

Mike sighed, then turned to Cathy. "You thirsty?"

She did nothing at first, then turned to glare at him. "No," she said finally, when he seemed oblivious to the meaning of her icy looks.

"You sure? I could run in and get you a Coke..."

"I'm fine."

"Okay, well, if you want anything..."

"I won't."

Mandy rolled her eyes again. "P.D.A." she said under her breath.

"What?" Mike asked, somewhere between annoyed and intrigued.

Mandy blushed a little when she realized she'd been heard. "Public Display of Aggression."

He laughed. "Yeah, I guess so. I was thinking more along the lines of Periodic Display of Assumption. I keep assuming that things are all right between me and her."

Mandy sighed, touched his arm gracefully, and sent shivers up his spine. "It's not."

"Hey, girls!" Tommy said loudly, breaking up the individual conversations (as well as Xander and Julie's kiss) as he entered the circle around the picnic table. "Whoa, Drew! Didn't mean to interrupt. If I'd had known, I would have brought popcorn."

"Hi, Tommy." Xander breathed, choosing to ignore the previous statement. "How are you?"

"Better now that I'm here," he said, giving Cathy the once over with his eyes, then spotting Mike alongside her. "Three guys, three girls... that spells orgy in my book."

"Well, like, it spells 'Threeguysthreegirls' in mine," Mandy smirked.

Tommy smiled, moving away from Cathy and Mike and over to Mandy. "Yeah," he agreed, nodding slowly. "Yeah, I guess that's true."

Mike stiffened.

Xander shot his friend a look, before turning to Tommy. "Hey, man. Did you take notes in History? That's where O'Toole's session fell this week and I need to make it up."

"No problem," Tommy agreed without even giving Xander so much as a glance, his gaze trained on Mandy. "So, what do you do all evening?" he asked her, his voice low and thick. He did not seem to notice that for every step he took toward her, Mandy was backing away two.

"Just homework, I write in my journal," she answered honestly, still stepping backward until she was against the table with nowhere to go.

"Do you ever write about me?"

"Sometimes."

"How about I come over sometime and give you something to write about." It wasn't phrased as a question, more like a demand.

"I don't think so," she said, laughing a little, although it was clear from the frantic look in her eyes and the beading sweat on her forehead that she didn't find the situation very funny at all.

"Why not?" he chided, stepping forward again, until now they were nose-to-nose. "I bet me and you could have some real fun..."

"Me too," Mike said, grabbing Tommy by the shoulder and pulling him away. He purposely put too much force behind it, sending the taller boy toppling to the damp grass, soaking the seat of his pants. "But you were right, you were interrupting something. Can me and Mandy finish our conversation now?"

Tommy looked up, his face a mixture of the hatred he felt toward Mike for ruining his moment, and shock that things had not gone as he'd planned; he wasn't fitting in after all, it seemed. "Sure," he said sarcastically, fixing the shirt collar that Mike had ruffled up. "No problem."

"Thanks," Mike replied, patting Tommy on the back and sending him on his way, then walking over to continue talking to Mandy.

Cathy glared at both of them as they started to talk again, her eyes turning bloodshot and teary.

"So," Tommy said, stepping up to her. "How about you? Did you enjoy yourself last night?"

"Go to hell, dirt-bag," she said simply, barely acknowledging his presence before she walked back toward the school.

Julie pulled Xander back in for another kiss. As she closed her eyes, he left his open for a moment, watching Mike and Mandy talk, Cathy walk away, and Tommy just sit there looking stupid.

Crossed the line, man, he sighed inwardly, wondering what his friend had gone and done now.

CHAPTER NINE:
BAD LATIN

Malcolm woke up on his couch around four.

He had let little Charles Frank take his bed, for obvious reasons. The child was magnificent, and deserved more than a night of late-night TV and butter-stained cushions.

He had not touched the child. Not last night. It hadn't been the right time. The child was too busy sucking on his candy to have wanted to suck on anything else, and Malcolm had enjoyed just chatting with the boy, finding out everything there was to know about him.

They'd both sat on Malcolm's bed talking until twelve when the boy had finally drifted off to sleep. Malcolm had carefully taken off the boy's clothes, leaving the underwear of course, that would be wrong. He folded the boy's tee-shirt and jeans and placed them on a nearby chair, as carefully as possible.

He did nothing else, but oh, he had wanted to.

He had felt himself grow and become hard in a way he could not remember having done in years as he pulled off the child's pants, revealing the wonder of his flawless, smooth body. Not a scar, not a scab. The boy was perfect, and soon would be perfect.

Malcolm had gone out to the couch and taken off all of his clothes, jumping under the dirty blanket he always left there. Slowly, he slid his hand underneath the covers and gripped what he found there, hard. He started to think of the boy, merely feet away. And the redhead that had so wanted him to see her, so that she could run home and do the same thing that he was doing now, if not better.

There was nothing wrong with that.

Maybe, after he was done being inside of the boy, either in the room or the woods, or maybe even against the couch, maybe he would take the boy out for a walk afterwards and the redhead would see them, and then the both of them could come home with him. Maybe she would show Malcolm her beautiful, silky body in exchange for seeing the boy's.

But she could not have him. There *would* be something wrong with that. The boy was only for him, his lips only for Malcolm's body, not some smutty teenager that wasn't even a blonde. No, she could not have him. But she could feast her eyes upon his naked form as he watched them. Yes, the boy would watch, naked for the girl, as Malcolm bent her over a chair, her dirty clothes in shreds on the floor.

That was the way it would have to be then. That was the way the boy wanted it. Charles not only wanted to have Malcolm, but to watch Malcolm conquer others. Wanted to watch as their useless, naked bodies tried to give Malcolm pleasure and failed. Then, as they watched and wished it were them, he would take the boy and then make them leave, touching the boy. Touching his privates gently, oh, so gently. Unless he wanted it to be rough.

Yes.

Maybe he wanted it to be rough. To play the game little boys played, when they said no and meant yes.

He waited, but the voice said nothing.

Finally, he burst, and he let out a long, pleasured howl of ecstasy, looking at the door where the boy would still be fast asleep.

CHAPTER TEN:
THE SLEEP

Xander clicked on the web browser at the top half of his screen, and to his surprise, it actually opened up.

"All right," he smirked, clapping once in celebration of himself. "Got my browser working, always a plus. That's all the operating system stuff stuff."

He opened a CD case that stood next to his monitor and began to flip through the shimmering disks one by one. "Now I just need to reinstall my games, redownload all my music and videos, and reestablish my entire web-cracking library. It only took me five years the first time."

He groaned, wanting to bash in his screen but deciding not to, as it had taken him almost two months to save for a new one from the last time his machine had frazzled on him.

A short beep came from his tower then, like a worker threatening his boss that he could strike again at any time. Xander responded as most employers would, by swiftly kicking the machine. It teetered once, then came back, resuming the pleasant humming sound it usually made.

"Still haven't fixed the problem of shutting you off..." he murmured to himself, as he grabbed a potato chip from a bag that had been open on his table for weeks and popped it into his face. He made a disgusted look, then moved the rest of the bag into the trash bin. "...every time I try start you up you go into safe mode. Why do you do that? I hate having to reroute every time, you stupid thing. Ugh."

He typed a command that opened his control panel and personal settings, fidgeting around with commands there.

"Can't be the Engen Virus... you're basically a completely new system. I flattened that hard drive, unless it was some kind of super-advanced trojan horse... no... why do you keep starting in safe mode?"

Because it can, he thought to himself, frowning as he continued to type away. *And you wish you could, too. Every time something goes wrong with the computer, every time it feels threatened in any way, it goes in to its safe mode and next to nothing can hurt it. It's protected... shielded, almost. I think it's one of the things computers do that we humans really admire. If we could do that, maybe our children wouldn't be as vulnerable. Maybe we'd be able to protect ourselves against the viruses out there. Maybe we'd actually have a clear shot at heaven.*

But I doubt it.

The computer made an odd groaning noise, and Xander glared at it.

"Quiet," he commanded, pointing at it dramatically. It continued making the noise, and Xander held the pose for a moment, feeling very stupid even though nobody could see him.

As if in deliberate defiance, the buzzing got louder.

"Judas," he said sardonically, shutting off the computer and reaching for his screwdriver. "I bet it's that damn CD Rom drive that Randy sold me that time. That son of a bitch..."

There was a knock at his bedroom door, and it gave Xander such a start that he dropped the screwdriver. He turned, then smiled a little as he realized who it was. He glanced over at his clock, realizing that it was six. She was early. That was a good sign, he assumed.

He walked to the door and unlocked it quickly, opening it wide. "Hey, Julie, you're..."

He stopped, giving Cathy an odd look as she gazed at him, holding her hands together in front of her waist. She was wearing the same pink sweater that she had been in class today, and the same loose jeans, even though they were considerably more wet. Her hair was soaked, and he guessed that she had gotten a shower and just decided that her old clothes would do. But her eyes were wet, too, smearing the make-up that looked like it had been applied in a hurry.

"You're not Julie." he said, but he was still smiling honestly. "Come on in, though. You were my second choice, I assure you."

She stepped in, taking a glance at the computer without a top cover on its tower. "I'm sorry if I disturbed you. Your Mom let me in," she said quietly, her voice harsh like she had a throat infection.

"It's no problem," he said, tilting his head at her.

She just stood there, looking down at the floor, standing perfectly still, one arm holding the other. Her black hair was even blacker now that it was damp, and the water weighed it down enough that it was pulled straight on either side of her face like twin lines, a stray hair curling wildly every now and again.

She kept staring at the floor, and he followed her gaze to try and figure out what she was staring at. The only thing he could find in her line of sight was a sock he'd missed when he cleaned up earlier, one that he thought might have gone missing from the last wash load. He made a mental check to pick it up before Julie arrived.

"Is something wrong?" he asked finally, craning his head down so that he could see her face, hidden by her hair.

As if on cue, tears started to fall from her eyes again and her arms came up to her face, shielding it from all the world. A pain-filled moan escaped from her lips, and nothing had ever hurt Xander quite as much.

"Oh, come here," he said softly, pulling her into his arms. Her face immediately found its home nuzzled under his chin as he wrapped his arms around her, holding her tight.

She still covered her face with her hands, not hugging back, just wanting to be held. Her entire body began to convulse as the tears overcame her, and when he knees began to wobble he led her over to the bed and sat her down.

"You're shivering," he noticed, wondering how he had not before. He grabbed the blankets off his bed and wrapped them around her, bundling her up as best he could. "Did you walk over here like that after a shower or something? Cathy, you'll catch your death of cold."

She spat something then, a word he didn't quite recognize.

"What was that?"

"Good," she repeated, a little louder this time.

He frowned, looking at her. He reached up, took her hair and pulled it behind her ear, caressing her face as he did so. "No, that would not be good," he informed her politely, even a little patronizingly. "Because you, you Cathy, you are my very favorite person of everyone I know. And that's saying something, because I'm a popular guy lately."

She smiled a little, but it wasn't a real one, and she was only fooling herself if she thought he bought it. "I guess," she said finally.

He moved closer to her and put an arm around her, letting her rest on his shoulder.

"What's wrong, Cathy?" he asked, his voice suddenly wiser despite his youth.

"It's Mike..." she started, sobbing a little as she said his name. "But it's not. It's me. It's everything about me. Why does it have to be this way? Why can't it all just go away? Why can't I be happy, Xander?"

He took a breath, letting out a respectful chuckle.

"That is a lot of questions," he said, giving her a little squeeze with his arm. "And the answer is... I really don't know. I wish I did, I really do. As near as I can figure, you're the person who gets punished when I mess up. I didn't notice Grendel, he hurt you. I didn't notice Phillips, he hurt you. Derek, he hurt you. I couldn't stop the Anti-Womb, and it hurt you. It seems like you're the thing that

God punishes to tell me, 'You're not fighting for yourself, y'know. Nobody that gets real power gets any choice'. I wish you didn't have to be. I wish I could do a better job of protecting you."

"You shouldn't have to!" she said, forcing the words out through involuntary whines made by a throat racked by tears. "But you still do. You do everything and still try to protect me. Mike's supposed to protect me, but he's too busy saving Mandy from someone asking her out on a date!"

"To be fair, Tommy was asking for..."

"I don't care!" she screamed, but not at him. "I want a boyfriend who'll protect me. Who'll never push and will be there when I need him and that I can go to anytime and feel safe in his arms! I want someone who will love me and hold me, and..." she sobbed, and her shoulder convulsed. She buried both her head and arms in his lap, letting out a painful wail that, if you were paying attention, had in it the words, "...and I want my baby!"

He shut his eyes tight when he heard that, several tears running down his cheeks. They dripped from his chin slowly and landed on her head.

She noticed them and sat up.

His lower lip quivered, but he wiped away the tears before she could see.

"Oh, Cathy," he said, looking at her red, puffy eyes and sniffing back moisture. "I am so sorry I can't make any of those things happen for you."

She started to cry again. "Yes, you can, I know you can."

"Honey, I wish I could..."

"You can," she said, almost a whisper. She moved forward, her lips found his.

She smelled like spring rain, that crispness in the air that followed a light shower, everything in nature clean and sharp. Her lips felt like silk on his and he leaned forward, opening his mouth to get more. His head screamed more, yelled at him to see how much of the silky feeling of her lips he could find with his own. Her tongue tasted tangy, like limes. He could hear her breathing and he felt that breath against his cheek.

Suddenly, he pulled back. "Um... Ju..." he stammered, raising a finger to stop her as she started to come forward again.

She smiled, and began to lean in again.

"Julie," he said finally, finding his wits. He sat up firmly and she sat up too, leaning back away from him. "Cathy, I'm with Julie. You're with Mike. He's my *best friend*."

"Yeah, right," she sighed, nodding. "Sure. Why not?"

"If it wasn't for that..."

"Got it," she said quickly, cutting him off as she stood up and started for the door.

"Cathy, you don't have to go," he said, rising and stepping between her and the exit.

"No, actually, I really do," she said finally, stepping around him. "Because both you and Mike have Peterson on the brain and I can't even... I thought you of all people... I love you so... and Mike, he..." she started to cry, turning from him and heading out the door without another word.

And for once, he let her go. He turned quickly and

kicked his computer, slamming it against the wall. It immediately started in safe mode.

"Lucky bastard," he cursed, closing his door and rubbing his hands through his hair as he sat on the edge of his bed.

ᚠ᚜ᚠ

Julie's gone out to meet Xander. Second night in a row they had a late-night date. Good for them, I guess. The sooner they get into dating, the sooner they can go at it. The sooner they go at it, the sooner they can break up.

Mandy had just gotten out of the shower, her hair still damp and pulled up into twin pig-tails on either side of her little face. She had switched from her pink, feathery pen to a more traditional Bic blue. It wasn't nearly as fancy, but she found it was easier to use. No feathers to tickle her nose, either.

That's the way these things happen, isn't it? Guy meets girl, they go at it, he leaves? I know that's not always the way it happens... but really, it is. Someone always leaves, someone always dies or divorces you. Better for it to happen sooner than later, as far as I'm concerned.

What's really unhealthy is what's going on between Mike and Cathy. It's bad enough when couples that are happy don't break up before they become, like, inevitably miserable, but they're already post-historic. Why do they keep up this dog-and-pony show when all they ever do is fight and make people uncomfortable?

Mike stood up to Tommy for me today, and it was great. He's such a sweet guy, and he deserves so much better than Cathy. He deserves better than me, too, but that won't stop me from trying. No way will that stop me from trying. He told me I looked pretty. And that he liked the way I danced. He told me that last night I looked like a little angel. A princess. Then he said I looked like the angel of a princess, and I laughed. He laughed too, because it was kinda funny. I guess you'd, like, have to have been there... or something.

Another kid went missing last night. That's two in two months, which is really creepy. The town is, like, talking about putting the curfew in again, which would be great. Really. But the kid was taken in broad daylight. What? Is curfew going to start at noon?

Nothing makes sense anymore. These past few days, it's like we've all just been floating around. Eventually, one of us is going to bump into another. I'm just going to make sure that, at the end of the day, I'm the one on top.

⋏⋏

Xander lay on his bed, staring up at the plain white ceiling he'd had ever since he could remember. Every big moment in his life was marked by a scar somewhere on the face of that room, a place that had seen the worst of his anger during times of trial.

He thought that those walls were very lucky, because they got to keep their scars.

He wasn't so lucky. He couldn't just look to a patch of white skin on his elbow and say, 'remember when I scraped that on my bike,' and then not look at it or think of it for months. No, his scars would heal. But with nothing to reference from, they came back to him over and over again, without rhyme or reason.

Cathy must feel the same way, he thought. *That must be*

why she acts the way she does, does the things she does. She's like me, she doesn't have the benefit of scars to go along with what she feels on the inside, because all of her damage is on the inside.

There was a very faint knock at the door. Xander leapt to his feet, turned the knob and opened it swiftly. It swung even faster than he had meant it to, and there she was, standing with both her hands holding her purse in front of her, looking like a top prize. She was wearing a loose navy sweatshirt that had a very wide neck, which she wore down over one shoulder, revealing a great deal of her upper arm. The shirt was cut off half way, showing off her navel and slender form before reaching the hip-hugger jeans that looked like they would have fit Mandy two years ago they were so tight. Her hair was in two identical downward pointing pigtails, drawing her hair back from her beautiful face. Foundation covered up most of her freckles, but a scattered few shone through beneath her soft, green eyes.

"Wow," Xander said, tearing his eyes from her long enough to look down at his plain black shirt and jeans. "Suddenly, I feel under-dressed."

She gave him a coy smile that he recognized all too well.

"You look great," she said honestly. "But, just for the record, I'd prefer you undressed to underdressed every day of the week and twice on Sundays."

Xander raised an eyebrow. "Every day of the week and twice on Sundays, huh? Can I get that in writing, maybe? Written contract, declaration of intentions..."

"Most of my intentions for you are illegal in forty-eight states," she responded, and she didn't look like she was joking, although she had always been good at making him squirm at just the right moment.

"What are the other two?" he asked, the sexual-undertone lost from his voice now, replaced by a genuine interest as he stepped closer to her.

"Alaska and Hawaii... the freak states," she laughed, wrapping her arms around his neck. "They'll let you do just about anything there."

"I see, I see," he replied, taking a deep, calming breath as he wrapped his hands around her waist. He pulled her body close to his until he could smell her perfume all around him and feel those pigtails caress his chin and chest. "So, how was your day?"

"All right. I thought I saw a raccoon outside my window, but it was just a really weird spotted cat."

"That's great."

She smiled, drawing her lips so close to his that they were a hair's width away from touching. "So, I think that's enough small talk for today, don't you?"

"Absolutely," he nodded, kissing her passionately as she pulled him onto the floor of his bedroom, their lips and hands dancing over each other wildly. They let themselves go like never before, neither of them afraid, neither of them worried, and both of them understanding.

ᛞ

They lay on his bed and watched *Mallrats*.

They'd already gone through *Clerks*, during all ninety-one minutes of which Julie had wondered why anyone would film a movie in black and white now that there was colour, unless it was set in World War Two. She also wondered what she'd done to Xander to make him angry enough at her to force her to watch a movie based on convenience store clerks and junkies.

"It's a cult classic," he told her again, smiling in disbelief that she really had not enjoyed the film.

"Apparently 'cult classic' means: 'nobody but idiots and obese people from New Jersey will like this film'."

"Hey," he started, waving a finger. Then he stopped himself, considered it, and lowered the finger. "Actually, for the most part, yeah, that's true. But *Mallrats* is good."

"The case says there's mild nudity in it," she said, reading the back of the neon green case. "And it had Jason Lee in it. He ruled in *Almost Famous*."

"Indeed he did," Xander said. He had no qualms about any film that could combine romance with rock and roll.

"How come none of the movies you like to watch have excessive nudity, or even, any nudity on the back? Seriously, would it kill you to rent a good porno to get me in the mood?"

He almost burst a gut at that, slapping his hand against the floor. "I think you and I both know that we're not trying to get each other 'on the go'. Wasn't the last hour rolling around on my floor playing and making out touchy-feely enough for you?"

She smiled devilishly and turned around from where she lay, giving him a kiss. "Not nearly."

He fought his cheek's urge to turn blazing red with embarrassment.

"Aww, look at the boy blush," she teased, reaching up and squeezing his cheek. "Isn't he cute?"

He smiled. "Yeah, yeah. Flattery will get you no-where."

"Got me this far. And honestly, I don't want to be any farther, yet."

"Me neither."

"I'm glad," she smiled, again leaning back on him.

There was a pause then as Ben Affleck punched some guy in the ribs and made a rude comment about his girl-friend, then Xander interjected. "Then what was with all the talk about porn?"

He felt her grin, although he couldn't see it. "Girl's gotta get her rocks off somehow, don't'cha know."

卂

Mike ran down the stairs as the knocking continued, more frantic than ever now, like the pounding of soccer balls against his front door.

"I'm coming!" he yelled, trying desperately to finish getting his shirt on as he ran. "At six am, this had better be..."

He opened the door. Cathy stared back at him, soaked to the bone, her lower lip quivering. She stared at him, and him right back at her for a long moment, until she stepped inside.

"We need to talk."

CHAPTER ELEVEN:
BLISS

He woke up first.

As his eyes blinked open, it took him a moment to process exactly why that had been his first waking thought of the new day. When he opened them completely, the answer was all too clear.

Julie was next to him, asleep with one of his arms still wrapped around her slender body, which had been stripped down to her undergarments late the night before. She promised him that she'd only wanted to sleep for a few minutes, a promise that the both of them had had every intention of keeping.

Xander had fallen asleep to the gentle sound of her breathing, the smell of her hair and the feeling of the silky skin of her body against his. She was quite possibly the most gorgeous thing he had ever seen right then, as he saw her from the other side of the morning light that came streaming in through his bedroom window.

The colour slowly drained from his face and he became haggard as he leaned closer to make sure she was still breathing. Putting a hand near her nose, he waited for what seemed like forever until she exhaled gently onto his palm, then breathed a sigh of relief.

What was I thinking? he cursed himself, slapping his forehead with his free hand. *Falling asleep with her next to me? If I had transformed, she would have been the first thing the Womb would have ripped into. She would have been lucky if she'd even gotten the chance to wake up.* He shuddered, trying to force that mental picture away. It lingered, hanging there at the base of his skull and haunting him.

It would have looked at her with those cold, aquatic eyes and it would have opened its mouth, hungry for her blood after all this time watching her from within Xander's consciousness. It would have gently rolled her over, gazed upon her supple breasts through that white, almost transparent bra she was wearing, and lapped out its tongue out to tickle her all the way down to her stomach. She would have started to wake then, giggling just a little. She may have even woken enough to playfully ask him to stop.

And it would.

It would have opened its mouth all the way, then dug into her with those great, sharp fangs, spraying her blood into its mouth as her eyes jolted open in pain and shock. She would have been so scared she wouldn't even have realized what was happening until she was very close to death. She'd have looked around for Xander and wouldn't find him, called out to him and he wouldn't come...

Argh! he yelled at himself inwardly. He slapped his head again, as if to knock the wicked thought from his skull and turned to look at her.

The makeup she had so carefully applied was smudged now, most of it having rubbed off onto his pillows or his shirt at some point during the night. Her freckles were all showing now, each one a slightly different size and shade than the one before it. They were snowflakes, each one of them unique.

He leaned over and kissed her carefully on the cheek, gentle enough not to wake her. She smiled warmly, and it made him feel good. Even her dreams were undisturbed by him. He hadn't so much as twitched. The Womb hadn't so much as twitched.

He thought back to the raspy words of Adam Genblade, when he'd first been told about the nature of The Womb.

"Because," came the voice from the darkness. "It's true. The Black Womb's consciousness resides within you. You have remarkable skills, my boy, but not even you can control it twenty-four hours a day. These past few months while you sleep, it escapes. It's easy to identify. When you call him, when you have his body surrounding yours and you still remain in control, your eyes have a reddish tint to them. But Black Womb's consciousness is let out when you stop thinking rationally, when you get extremely emotional, or when you sleep..."

When he realized what was happening he stopped, the anger fading from his face. O'Toole, although he couldn't possibly know it, was right. Emotion was a major trigger of the Black Womb. If he almost transformed out of anger... there was nothing saying that strong emotions caused by Julie couldn't do it too. Slowly, he nodded. "You're right."

ᚠᚤᚠ

when you get extremely emotional
Emotion was a major trigger of the Black Womb.

Xander looked at Julie again and it was different than the happiness he had felt first when he had woken next to her. He didn't feel the fear and anger when he had realized what he could have done. What he felt was sadness. He wanted to be so sad that his eyes welled up and glossed over tears, but they didn't. His eyes remained dry, if ever sorrowful, as he looked upon her beautiful face.

"The Womb never stirred," he whispered to himself, slowly sliding his arm out from under her body and sitting up, all of the blood draining from his face. "Didn't twitch, didn't even flinch. It just..." he fought it, trying to think.

Maybe it had happened. Maybe he had transformed, and he just hadn't realized, and the Womb had not killed Julie, maybe--

"No," he said, arguing with the part of his mind that was trying frantically to come up with explanations. "No, there's no blood. I don't have the layer of blood on me. It wasn't there, always was before. So, I couldn't have transformed."

He sighed as he turned back toward her, then reached out and caressed her naked arm, so smooth and delicate.

"I couldn't have transformed," he repeated softly, almost like an apology.

If I had transformed, I would have killed her, he reminded himself, but that feeling of dread still would not go away. *But emotion is one of the best, most effective ways to get me to* turn Womb. *If I didn't feel enough kissing her... sleeping next to her... waking up with her... to even make it twitch, then I feel nothing for her. No love, no bliss... not even happiness, not really.*

He turned away from her, again wanting to cry. But he simply wasn't that sad about it, about knowing that he couldn't love her... no matter how hard he wanted to. No matter what way he tried to look at it, the emotion wasn't strong enough to make him twitch, let alone transform.

He brought both his hands up to his eyes, pressing against them until he saw spots.

So, he thought to himself. *To summarize, by sleeping next to her I was either going to kill her (proving that I loved her), or not kill her (proving that I can't love her).*

He frowned, burying his head in his hands and wishing to sob, but couldn't. He forced a fake one out, just for his own peace of mind. It didn't help.

"Xander?" came the soft voice, like the coo of a dove as it greeted the morning dew on the leaves around it.

He turned around to see her sitting there, the blankets pulled up around her to cover herself. Her hair had been taken down out of its pigtails long ago, and now dangled in front of her face in loose strands. She looked chubbier than usual, but definitely not unattractive. It was just a trick of light, but it made her look cute. She looked at him in near-nude innocence, her eyes half asking if anything had happened and half begging for something to happen. She had never looked so beautiful in all the months he'd known her, since he first spotted her at the party.

And still, he felt nothing.

"What time is it?" she asked, her voice scratchy with

that mid-morning film one got when they hadn't brushed their teeth the night before. She glanced back at his door to make sure that it was locked, then stood up on his floor and let the blankets fall, casually walking around in her bra and underpants, perfectly comfortable with him.

"Um," he grunted, shaking the cobwebs out of his head as he turned toward his clock. "Quarter to nine."

"Did I stay here all night?" she asked, turning toward him and smirking.

"Yea, sorry about that." he apologized, scratching the back of his head and avoiding eye contact.

"Don't be," she said flatly, without any trace of sarcasm or taunting. She turned and walked toward him, still half-naked.

He gulped back hard, knowing what must be coming.

"I've never... it's been a long time since I woke up without being scared, without having to worry... I've never felt so safe, not even in my own bed, in my own house, with all my doors locked shut, as I did in your arms last night."

He forced a smile. "I... liked it too," he managed, his voice wavering with each syllable as his eyes darted from hers, on down to the rest of her slender, exposed body.

She smirked. "If it's all the same to you, though, do you think I could get dressed now?"

"Yeah," he said simply, getting up. "I will too."

She gave him the once over with her eyes, forcing him to look down at himself and realize that he had not gotten undressed when he had crawled into bed with her last night.

"Look at that," he said with obvious mock-cheerfulness. "Done already. What's taking you?"

"Very funny," she said, turning to pick up her pants. She slapped her hip playfully, giving him a look from between her legs as she bent over.

He turned away and found a point on his wall to stare at while she got ready.

She pulled on her jeans, looking up at him as she hopped into them. Her eyes became confused, squinting and tilting up as they met with his. She raised an eyebrow at him.

He tried to ignore her, but she pressed the matter. "What's wrong?" she asked. She closed the few steps between them as she pulled on her sweatshirt and touched her palm against his face. "Is something the matter?"

"No," he said hoarsely, turning toward the door. "I just don't want to be late for school."

"Since when?" she asked, folding her arms and almost giggling.

"Look, really, it's nothing. I just..."

"Oh," she laughed, "I know."

He turned white as he faced her, his posture sinking. "You do?"

"Yeah, Alex." she smiled, leaning in and kissing him lightly on the lips. "I know you, remember? You're all into the emotional side of things..."

His eyes went wide. He could see where this was going. "Oh, no. See, that's not it."

"You don't have to lie to me, Mr. Drew. I wouldn't ever lie to you. I feel better with you than anyone else, and last night was the best night of my entire life. Nothing else has ever come close."

"Julie, please..."

"I love you, Alex," she said, gazing deep into his eyes, happily serious. Her eyes shone big and bright, sparkling in anticipation of his response.

There was a long pause as he met her gaze. She waited.

Hoped.

Prayed.

And with each passing second the light left her eyes a little more until there was barely any left, but she still met his stare until he broke it, turning away.

"I..." he started, hoping that the words would do something. But still, even at this moment, the True Womb refused to budge. For once, it refused to even answer his desperate call. "I can't."

It was like a bomb had been dropped on her soul as the last of the light vanished from her eyes, only to be replaced by a new sparkle: the sparkle of tears being held back as they filled her vision. "Right," she said, grabbing her purse and motioning for him to join her down the stairs as they started off to school.

"Julie, I'm really sorry," he pleaded, reaching out for her.

She moved to avoid his grip, turning back to him. "No, really. It's cool. I... I don't either. I was just saying it so that you'd feel better. I'm sorry, I just..." she trailed off, her voice becoming very wavering. When it returned it had a firm resolve he hadn't heard from her in weeks. "...I just thought it was what you'd want to hear." She sniffed once, then turned toward the door. "Come on, we gotta get going."

He nodded, then followed her down his stairs and out the door, begging the entire time for his heart to break.

But it didn't.

"Are you okay?" he asked her for the third time.

This time she looked up, only now noticing him.

"Oh, yeah. Sure, I guess," she said. She pulled the blanket he had given her closer around her, trying to keep what little body heat she had in.

"Would you like some more covers? There's plenty up on my bed." Mike offered, motioning up the stairs and even starting to get up to go grab them for her.

"No thanks," Cathy murmured. She reached out from between the covers and picked up the hot tea he'd just poured up for her and brought it to her lips. "And I remember, by the way."

He sighed, his shoulders slumping.

Then, suddenly, he chuckled.

"Yeah," he responded, sitting down next to her as he twirled the spoon in his own tea. "Yeah, I guess you would, huh?"

"Not the kind of thing you forget," she half-grinned, her eyes meeting his for a second.

There was a long pause as they both played with their tea.

"I'm really sorry," he said finally, dropping the spoon with a clang.

"About what?" she asked, not as a surprised question but more as a test to make sure he wasn't just saying it.

"For everything," he responded painfully, taking her off guard. "For the way I reacted, for the things I said when you told me you were pregnant... for the way I've been behaving ever since..." he groaned. "For breaking us so soon after we finally got ourselves fixed. For not trying to fix this sooner. For waiting for you to make the first move, when I should have been on your doorstep the next day with chocolates and flowers and, and, and a new car."

"I can't drive."

"Neither can a lot of people in our class, but they still do."

She chuckled.

"Thank you," she said honestly, meeting his gaze for more than a second for the first time since she'd arrived.

There was a long pause and Mike resisted the impulse to pick up his spoon and start playing with it again. There was already a growing puddle of tea around his cup and he hadn't taken so much as a sip yet.

"And just for the record," she said, sighing deeply. "It took the both of us to break this relationship, and it took both of us to keep the other from taking that first step."

He thought about that for a moment, then nodded. "You know," he said carefully, praying that he wasn't pushing things. "As first steps go, I'd say this isn't too shabby."

She grinned at him. "Not too shabby at all."

Both sets of eyes went back to the tea.

"About what happened... I should have been there for you," he said.

Slowly, carefully, she reached out to him and touched his hand. "We should have been there for each other.

Since it died, I've just felt like everything is wrong. Tainted, somehow."

"I know that feeling. I've been having it all month."

She sighed. "I know it might seem that long... gawd, it does to me too, but it hasn't been..."

"I've been feeling it ever since you cut me out. Ever since we made love, and you just shut me out. You didn't let me talk to you, you didn't call, you avoided me... what was I supposed to think?"

"Shh..." she soothed, rubbing his hands. She nodded quickly, over and over again. "I know, I know, baby. We both made mistakes. But... it can be better now, can't it?"

He swallowed hard, choking on unshed salt water.

"I don't know," he answered finally, looking away from her.

Her mouth dropped, and she looked as though she could not breathe. "Oh."

"It's not that I don't want to," he said hastily, his eyes filled with panic. "But there's been so much pain, so much hurt done to us and done by us... how can we ever make it right again?" He laughed then, and she gave him a quizzical look. "You wanna know something stupid?"

She shook her head. "I'm sure it won't be stupid."

"I've been naming it."

Her eyes went wide. "What?"

"It. Our baby."

"I know, but what do - "

"Girl names, boy names... doing lists. Trying to have something to pin my grief to, y'know? Trying to..."

"Trying to give it a home so you can visit it, instead of just keeping it in the front of your mind at all times."

He looked at her, perplexed.

"I do it, too," she said, stepping off her chair and kneeling down close to him. "Oh, gawd, I do it every other minute."

Mike sniffed, the tears flowing freely now, as he drove his head into her breast. "And that story in the Daily about how the Walker parents can't afford to put Kerri's name up on the wall, and now this little boy has been missing for days and... oh, my god, Cathy... what kind of a world is this to bring a child into anyway?"

She nodded, her eyes growing wide. "I know, baby. I know. It's terrible."

"But we can do it," he sniffed, coughing.

"What do you mean?"

"We can fix it," he said, taking his head from out of her shirt and lacing their fingers together. A lover's grip that she did not fight. "We can make it better. We can make the world better, make it a place fit to bring a child into. And then, someday, we can do that, too."

She took him into her arms and kissed him. Tears streamed from their eyes as hot as any passion ever felt, and they were never more sure of where they belonged or of who they belonged to.

She chuckled a little while they held one another on his dining room floor, as their tea got cold.

"What?" he asked, kissing her neck briefly.

"I just wish I'd come to you first," she laughed, returning the favor and kissing him on the neck.

"Why?" he smiled, moving back so that he could look into her amazing eyes once more. "Who did you go to first?"

CHAPTER TWELVE:
GRUDGE

The boy had asked to go home again, playing the game where he pretended not to like it here. Pretended not to want Malcolm, saying no when he meant yes. He had told him no, that he could not go home just yet. To wait a little while longer, or his mother would get mad.

The boy was hungry; he could see that.

"Would you like some cereal?" Malcolm asked, smiling at the boy. "I have Frosted Flakes."

The boy nodded, wiping his eyes and smiling at his new friend. Malcolm smiled back, winking at the child. See, there? He wanted to stay, he just wanted something for it, like any young boy.

Malcolm led the boy to the table and turned on the porno that the obese man at the store had rented him, telling the boy to watch it. He went into the kitchen and opened the cupboard, taking out the Frosted Flakes and milk, as well as and a bottle of extra strength Aspirin. He dumped the remainder of the bottle into the bowl and poured the milk in, stirring it until the pills had dissolved completely.

This was the way the boy wanted it. He wanted to wake up and know what had happened, and then he would want it again.

There was nothing wrong with that.

⋏⋎⋏

Xander sat by the brick wall at the far side of the school, puffing on his cigarette. The smoke was stale and hurt his throat, but he ignored it. Although his body did not want it right now, his mind was craving the satisfaction of holding it in his hand and watching the smoke swirl up from it into the air all around.

How did everything get so messed up? he wondered to himself, as he watched each strand of smoke until it disappeared in the fall air. *I thought everything was going perfect. Everything was all right. What happened? Maybe it wasn't okay to begin with. Maybe I just didn't let myself see what was wrong, so that I might actually have a shot at being happy or knowing some peace.*

I guess what they say is true. Ignorance is bliss.

He took another puff, closing his eyes to enjoy it as the smoke traveled down into his lungs, ripped away at flesh as it went. It burned at his insides until the desired reaction was reached and his craving ceased.

Suddenly, pain erupted from the left side of his head, and he felt himself lift briefly from the ground only to meet it again, face first. Gravel stuck into his cheek and old cigarette butts crammed into his mouth, his smoke flying into the grass. The moist greens smoked a little before the cherry extinguished itself.

He growled a little, deep inside his throat. He turned his blood and grime-soaked face to see who had assaulted him just in time to see the sneaker come at him again. This attack would have driven a normal person's nose into their brain, killing them instantly, but on Xander it only felt that way. Blood gushed immediately from both nostrils, making the stench of smoke that had irritated them before seem as sweet as roses as his senses were overwhelmed by the coppery taste and stench of blood. The healing factor sputtered to life deep within his gut, taking a moment to gather itself, as if it, too, had been taken by surprise.

"What the hell?!" Xander screamed. His vision slowly returned to him as he tried to get to his feet. He raised his hands this time before turning in his aggressor's direction, afraid to pop his claws for fear that it was some punk kid like Tommy or Randy.

When his vision cleared, Mike was standing before him. His shoulders were hunched and his fists were clenched.

Xander wiped the blood from his lower jaw, rising to his feet to meet his friend's eye. "Mike? What the fuck is the matter with you, man?"

Mike drew back and slammed his fist into Xander's right cheek, sending saliva spattering against the wall of the school, followed by Xander.

Xander slid to the ground, his gums ripped to shreds by the brick.

Mike drew back his foot again and connected it as hard as he could with Xander's side.

There was a wet snap as Xander felt his ribs part, followed by an even sicker, longer moist crack as the healing factor pushed it back into place before it could puncture an organ. "Mike, why are you -"

Mike picked up a large rock in his right palm and slammed it against his friend's head, driving the pointed granite deep into the base of his neck.

Xander screamed, long and loud, having to bite down on his lip until it bled to stop himself. His eyes bruised almost instantly, darkening from the continuing grievances being slammed against it.

"What did I do?" he bellowed. Mike responded only by pummeling him with the rock, which now felt more like a small boulder. It landed in roughly the same spot he had the first time, forcing Xander flat against his belly.

Mike stepped onto his friend's back, curling his lip in hatred and disgust. He knelt down to his shivering, bleeding compatriot and grabbed a clump of hair, pulling back and stretching the neck until he heard the calcium within it pop. Then Mike gave one last, hard tug before bringing back his leg again, kicking him at the point where the skull met the neck, driving Xander back down into the gravel.

He stood there, breathing heavily on his friend's back for a moment, his fists clenched so tightly that they were turning white and stinging. His breathing got heavier, showing no sign of calming down.

There was almost as much blood as there was mud on the ground now; the resulting colour was sickening, like a mix of everything that you didn't want coming out of your body at once.

Mike kicked him in the side, making Xander's body jolt.

"Argh!" Xander bellowed.

Mike kicked again, this time getting the desired result as Xander rolling over onto his back. He bent over and forced his knees into Xander's ribs, bending them inward until he heard the snap. He grabbed Xander by the collar and pulled him up, his head hanging against the back of his shirt.

Mike drew back his arm and punched, slamming as much force as he could into Xander's jaw. Then he did it again. And again. The third time, he let go of the collar, letting Xander fall to the ground. He leaned over, grabbed his friend around the throat and pushed both of his thumbs into his adam's apple as hard as he could, smiling as he felt them sink in deep.

Xander's hands shot up as quick as mercury, grabbing Mike around both wrists. His eyes opened, revealing that the black his pupils had finally taken over, rendering them an opaque ebony that reflected Mike's face back at him.

"That's about enough," he said, grunting as his vocal cords were pressed even tighter. With four sickening sequential -thunks!-, he impaled all eight of his finger-bound talons into his friend's arms, sending tiny spurts of blood from both of them as the razor sharp implements sliced through both sets of flesh.

"Ah!" Mike grunted, gritting his teeth together before mentally bundling the pain into a tiny ball and throwing it into the back of his stomach where it belonged. He tried to pull away, loosening his grip on Xander's throat, but the claws were still inside him, dangerously close to vital veins. Pursing his lips and puffing out his cheeks, he took one long, frustrated breath then pulled away, making the claws rip the remainder of the way down his arms and out through his palms.

Xander's heart pumped faster, aching within his chest, and the true womb began to bleat and churn, rolling over like a sea-sick gut.

"You..." Mike snarled, holding both of his arms against his chest in a vain effort to stop them from hemorrhaging. "You of all people. I *trusted* you, and you did *that*."

The Womb sprang to life, flowing into Xander's veins, traveling through his entire body in the span of a few seconds and increasing his blood pressure until it felt as though he were going to suffer a heart attack and an aneurism all at the same time.

"I don't know what you're talking about!" Xander pleaded, his voice corrupting into a more feral, bestial growl.

"Cathy!" Mike screamed at him, thrusting his hands outward as he gave into the rage pumping through him. His blood spilled against the walls and ground as he swung wildly at his friend, without any of the calculated hits he'd been performing before.

The pressure inside his body was finally too much, as both of Xander's wrists burst in tiny, red and black explosions, followed by an eruption on the left side of his neck. Spouts of blood splashed down over his body like a living thing, swirling about as though the liquid had an agenda all its own, covering every inch of Xander's form. Xander's mouth opened wide in a silent scream as the black ooze traveled upward, taking over his head and face.

For a long moment he stood there, like a statue of a dark shadow. Three curved, red lines appeared on his face, each opening to reveal strangely shaped eyes and a mouth full of razor sharp teeth that protruded from everywhere in his stained, putrid gums.

"Black Womb lives!" the creature bellowed so loudly that everyone inside the school must have heard.

Mike grinned, regarding the thing that nightmares were made of with an odd, detached chuckle. "I was beginning to wonder when you'd show up," he smiled, wiping a bit of blood from his face onto his sleeve. "Now the party can really start."

Black Womb stood stalwart and still, waiting for Mike's attack.

It came without a moment's notice, as Mike picked up a hunk of gravel and butts and hurled it into the Womb's large, scarlet eyes.

"Argh!" the Womb yelled, bringing Its hands up to Its eyes, accidentally sticking the claws in as It did so, drawing blood and impairing his vision. The healing factor took a moment to snap to attention, as if caught with its pants down.

When it opened its eyes, Mike's fist was less than an inch in front of It.

The blow struck hard, avoiding where the nose would be and taking advantage of the creature's sloped facial structure, hitting It between the eyes on a downward angle. The blow forced The Womb's yellow top teeth through their gums. A moment later the healing factor pushed the teeth back out, the action bringing the pain back anew.

"What the hell?" Xander screamed through the Womb's form, unsure of which part of his face to clutch in pain first.

"Don't look so shocked," Mike snarled, drawing back a heel, this time connecting with the soft patch of skin where he knew there were missing ribs from months earlier, connecting with the weakened true womb organ. He smiled as It howled in pain in three separate voices. "We've done this dance before, you and me... this has been coming since the first time you made googly eyes at my girlfriend."

From the ground, the Womb's head turned up and smiled, a sickening look on the beast. "Just so you know, she was the one who started with the googly eyes thing. I just wanted to be friends, scouts honor. But you know Cathy..."

Mike yelled, hurling his right fist through the air.

But this time Xander was ready for it, catching it in front of his face and digging the claws into each of Mike's tight, white knuckles, drawing blood and scratching bone with a sound like nails on a dry chalk board.

"Screw..." Mike started, but Xander squeezed harder, cutting off the snide remark.

Xander pulled back on his arm, forcing Mike's entire body forward, his head butting into the Black Womb's as hard as possible. There was a suckling sound as both their skulls ached under the pressure, and only the Womb's healed right away. Mike was left clutching his forehead.

"You!" Mike finished, kicking one of his legs from behind him and connecting with the Womb's calves, sending it toppling to the ground with rocks driving into its shoulders. "You knew what she meant to me! How could you?!"

"I didn't!" Xander coughed as he got up, black liquid

foaming around his mouth. "I swear! She came to me, you idiot! Because you went and pushed the line too far with Mandy, she had to come to me! She was confused!" he sprang to his feet, punching Mike in the left cheek, sending his friend back against the brick wall.

"I hate you..."

"She couldn't go to you, and you couldn't help her, because you were both being stupid! So, yeah, she came to me. And, guess what? I turned her down!"

He lashed out, all the pain and frustration of the past few hours leaking out through his fists, slamming Mike in the teeth as he tried to talk, chipping one in the back.

"I didn't want to! I would have given anything just a month ago! But it's different now. Everything's different! I didn't say no because of me, or because of Julie, and certainly not because of Cathy... it was you, you idiot! You stay with her even when you two aren't together, but no other guy is allowed to even LOOK! Not me, not Tommy, nobody!"

He attacked again, this time swiping his claws so close they ripped Mike's shirt in three places.

"Well, guess what, pal, it's time to pick a station or get off the train, cause I'm sick of this bullshit from you."

He slacked off then, letting his arms go limp at his sides.

Mike started to get up, this time raising an open palm in surrender... which quickly closed into a fist that jutted directly at the Womb's solar plexus, knocking It back at least a foot.

"It's not just Cathy, you moron!" he bellowed as the Womb fought Its way to Its feet. "You've been so wrapped up in your little life, you forget what's going on out there!

Peterson on the brain? You think I crossed the line with Mandy?" The confidence that had dominated his voice while he had been hurling insults had ebbed, a shake to each word replacing it. "While you're cuddling it up with Julie, there's a boy out there being kidnapped by some pervert two blocks from your house! What were you doing then, huh? Playing doctor with O'Toole, or trying to cop a feel from Peterson? Or was it the other way around?"

The Womb's claws shot forward, this time connecting with flesh as both parties staggered backward. "I've tried, dammit! I can't be everywhere, and I'll fucking try to kill myself again soon if this keeps up! I can't do everything, can't know everything! I'd give anything to be ignorant, don't you get that?"

Darkness fell over them then, as a man came down from above, landing with the grace of a ballet dancer directly between them.

The man stood up with his hair still perfectly placed despite the fall, in two perfectly straight lines on either side of his face. He wore black robes accented by ribbons, highlighting patterns that looked like Egyptian symbols. His milky facial skin was all that was seen of him, and even that was partially covered by linen bands that lapped his forehead, a small crystal caught in its center. Two more like it were found on similar bands, ceremoniously wrapped around each wrist.

"I don't," he said simply, as if the answer the Womb's question.

The man turned swiftly, raising a cane from beneath his cloak and whipping it into Mike's face, sending him to the ground with a face full of dirt and grime.

He turned then to the Black Womb, preparing to execute the same maneuver. He stopped and tilted his head slightly to the left, examining the creature.

"A darkness," he said casually, leaning the cane against the wall. "Interesting."

He brought both of his palms up to his forehead until the three gems were in line, and the blue one at the fore front sparkled for a moment before he brought them back down.

The Womb lunged and the man looked up, as if only now taking interest.

He smiled, a look that seemed odd on his colourless lips, reaching out and grabbing the Womb by both shoulders and spinning him in midair until his back was facing him. He brought his thumb and forefinger up to and pitched a muscle between the Womb's right shoulder.

All at once, faster than it ever had, the Womb splashed off of Xander's body as if it had the consistency of water rather than tar. There wasn't even a layer of blood covering his skin, and Xander was left with the bizarre feeling of disorientation, his world spinning before him. He wanted very much to vomit, then realized that the layer of blood had somehow retracted into his stomach.

"What did you do?" Xander gasped, coughing violently.

"A simple nerve pinch," the man responded, again picking up his cane. He drew it back, cracking Xander over the head with it. "You will be able to utilize your darkness again in a few scant hours. In the meantime..." he turned, again beating Mike across the face with his cane, who had been sneaking up behind him.

"Who are you?" Mike flouted, wiping blood from his eye.

"I, am Sebastian LeGaea," he said matter-of-factly, sticking his cane into the ground dramatically and striking a pose. His Scandinavian accent shone through thick when he said his own name, making it sound proud and majestic.

"And that means what to me?" Mike almost chuckled, nursing his broken cheek.

LeGaea's eyes narrowed, turning to really look at the boy for the first time since he had arrived. "It would mean a great deal, I assure you, were you not an ignorant pup pining over some teenage female."

"He's got a point, Mike," Xander murmured from the other side of their attacker.

"Shut up," Mike retorted, making a face.

"Enough. I grow sick of the both of you," LeGaea announced, as though it was God's decree then that they stop talking.

"Yeah, that oughta do it. Don't deal with teenagers much, do ya, Sebby?"

"Infidel," LeGaea cursed, turning and taking a step toward Mike now, a touch of vibrant red added to his pale cheeks.

As he spoke, Xander, still hazy, squinted at the gem on the man's right hand. It was large and red, and in any other place would have looked like one of the gaudy pieces of jewelry that Mandy wore. And yet, it looked almost familiar. "Is that..."

The Spider-Gem. The one and only. He could never not recognize it, now that it was in plain, unobstructed view. That was it. That gem was taken from Spider's sword, a woman Xander had killed in the heat of battle, which started the blood feud between he and Adam Genblade.

"If I were not in a rush, I would take the time to tear your eyes out and - "

"Guess what?" Xander asked.

When LeGaea turned, the boy was directly behind him.

"I'm feeling better."

He lashed out, punching LeGaea clear across the face. At the same moment, Mike kicked out both his feet, striking the robed man in both knee caps at once. He went down with a hard thump, followed by the rustling of settling fabrics.

Xander reached out and grabbed the Spider-Gem from LeGaea's outstretched palm, ripping the linen cloth as he did so.

"No!" Sebastian wailed, his eyes suddenly becoming bloodshot, like a junkie relieved of his last fix. "That's mine!"

Xander raised an eyebrow. "Have you looked up the definition lately?"

LeGaea lunged at Xander with both arms, trying the retrieve the gem.

Xander pulled back, but the man caught it with his left hand, maneuvering his head to try and yank it away. For the briefest of moments, all three gems touched.

"Run!" Mike yelled, as he forced Cathy ahead of him. The

creature landed on all fours on the sidewalk. His glossy eyes studied their movements, how they ran. He found their weak spot at the sides. They'd both been damaged there. It moved like a jaguar, leaping to the sidewalk and then onto two legs to pursue them.

"Keep... going..." Mike encouraged Cathy, holding his side. They were almost to her house. But they'd both danced this dance before. He wasn't about to make the same mistakes twice. He cut through an old alley, hoping to run across the backyard of the complex until reaching her back door. They could see the house now.

"Mike..." Cathy pleaded, grasping at her side. "It hurts."

Images of three girls crying, of a blonde woman holding her child, covered with blood. Tears are streaming down her face. I try to reach out to her, but my hands... they're knives. I keep trying to reach out, to help her... hold her... but I just keep cutting her. Stabbing at her until, eventually, they both die. A brunette, a blonde and a baby, dead in a pool of blood at my feet, and all I can do about it is keep reaching out...

Tom Petty blaring on a loud speaker. Too loud. Burning air. Pop tarts. Red. Blood red. Red. Red hair. Hurt. Pain. Hurt pain. Scream: too loud! Shattered. To ground. Look up. Smell of cream. Touch. Hair. Cheek. Grinding teeth. Death. Death! DEATH!

The blond boy's shirt came off with ease, tugging just a little

at the end, around the fingertips. His body was plump and per-
fect, just as it had been imagined. Death. Tiny nipples. Freckles,
lots of freckles. Something happening outside, no matter. The
door. The door!

⋀⋏

Sara's lips twitched as they turned blue, her body struggling
to suck in air as she fought for life. An inaudible word passed
through her lips. She cringed. Her body went limp as Genblade
breathed her in. His jagged teeth rattled as he brought his lips to
her face, his breath smelling like the sole of an old shoe.

"You taste like strawberries," he said finally, letting her fall
to the floor.

⋀⋏

She was crouching over him in a way a woman wearing
a dress like hers typically didn't. It was a red dress with long
slits up either leg, the fabric draping down and hanging in the
arc she'd formed between her legs. She wasn't wearing shoes,
he realized with an odd fixation, staring at manicured toes that
stood atop jagged, sloping rock. Her hair, long and blonde, fell
down over her shoulders in tumbling curls, just as it had on the
security footage he had twice seen her on now.

There were children close to her, so close they made him
uncomfortable. They were clothed in shirts too small for them
and dotted in filth, and each of them had visible scabs: the sort
that lingered and kept getting reopened and became a puss-filled
gangrenous sore by the time it was dealt with. She turned from
him and walked to the nearest group of children, a group of four
that looked to have a mean age of ten, and one larger boy who
seemed much older.

*She brought her nails to him and ran them over his skin,
then up through his hair, in a way that looked similar to that
which Cathy had touched Mike, but was different – it was one of
those rare human interactions where intent shone through, and
in this the intent was possession. In one fluid motion she had
told him everything he needed to know about her relationship
to these children.*

*When she laughed, it shook him even into the coldest reach-
es of his soul.*

ᚱ᚛ᚺ

LeGaea looked up at Xander, shocked.

Equally shocked, Xander stood in bewilderment for a
moment, then shook it off as sweat began to pour across
his brow, making it silky and smooth. As he came to his
senses, he ripped the Spider-Gem away from Sebastian,
drawing back a foot and kicking him under the chin. Le-
Gaea flew into the air and crashed to the ground back-
first, grunting uncharacteristically as he did so.

Mike swerved to miss him, then turned and eyed the
second gem, the gem of Aberdean, strapped to the villain's
left hand. He raised his sneaker high, bringing it down on
the crystal and cracking it, right down the middle.

"No!" LeGaea cried in shock, blood gushing suddenly
from his nose and mouth. "I am Sebastian LeGaea!"

"And I'm Mike Harris," he smirked. "Deal with it."

He kicked again, connecting with the bleeding man's
face.

LeGaea hit the ground, this time getting up quickly,
running toward the fence and leaping over it with ease.
He took off down the street and into the alley behind

Clarke's convenience.

"Dammit!" Mike cursed, trying to keep a visual bead on their attacker. "Where the hell did he go? We have to follow him!"

"No," Xander said, and the word sounded like a gasp.

Mike turned to see Xander, propping himself against the wall on the school, one hand holding the Spider-Gem and the over clutching his ribs, fighting for air. "Are you okay?"

"I'll be fine in a minute," Xander assured him, trying to convince himself more than Mike. "But we gotta go."

"Go?" Mike asked quizzically, throwing up his arms. "Go where, exactly?"

Xander looked up, and his eyes were filled with anger and hatred.

The blonde boy's shirt came off with ease, tugging just a little at the end, around the fingertips. His body was plump and perfect, just as it had been imagined. Death. Tiny nipples. Freckles, lots of freckles. Something happening outside, no matter. The door. The door!

"I know where he is."

CHAPTER THIRTEEN:
THE WORST THING

The boy had gone out like a light. It hadn't even taken as long as he thought. For a moment, Malcolm wondered if he had given him too much. That maybe his boy prince would expire, and not know the sublime pleasure of waking up next to Malcolm, knowing that he had been inside him and feeling happy for the first time in his young life.

The boy probably didn't have a father, he had decided at some point while watching young Charles Frank gobble down his special Frosted Flakes.

He reached out to the space near the boy's upper lip, waiting to feel the air come forth. After a moment it did, and Malcolm breathed a sigh of relief. He let his hand glide down an inch, finally getting to touch his finger against the boy's soft, silky lips. They were so smooth and fragile, not even that snobby teenager had lips like these, he decided.

Charles had enjoyed the dirty video that Malcolm had gotten from the obese man at the store even though there weren't any blondes in it. But there was nothing wrong with that. Charles was blonde enough.

Don't do that, Malcolm.

The voice said. It had returned an hour ago, as Charles had been eating his cereal. He had ignored it previously, but now he yelled, "Shut up, you bitch!"

The child did not stir, and Malcolm smiled as the voice ceased.

The child liked the movie, so he decided that he would bring the teenager over... maybe tomorrow, after Charles had woken up. Maybe after the boy let Malcolm play with his dirty parts for a little while, moaning the way Malcolm had the previous night while thinking of Charles. Yes, the boy wanted it. And the boy was letting Malcolm take his perfect body, so Malcolm would repay him with the girl, whether she wanted to or not.

He had to, to please the boy.

There was something happening outside, but it didn't matter.

He grabbed the boy's tee-shirt gently, pulling it over his head. It came off easily, except right at the end, when the boy's fingers got wrapped around the cloth. Even then, it took only a minute.

The boy's body was perfect and beautiful in its simplicity. It was splendid, and yet delicate.

There was a creaking sound, but he ignored it. The boy was all that mattered now.

His navel was an in, and that was something he was thankful for.

Don't do it, Malcolm.

Shut up, he thought, pushing the voice into the back of his mind where she belonged.

There were freckles on his body, and they seemed to make shapes like in the stars. What were they called? Constellations. The boy's freckles made tiny constellations across his body: of lions and tigers... and one of Malcolm, he was certain.

That decided it. The boy was made for him.

Don't do it, Malcolm, the voice chided.

Then he heard the noise again, somewhere near, but far away.

"Shut up, all of you."

He undid the button of the boy's jeans, preparing to remove them as well.

DON'T DO IT, MALCOLM!

"Shut up, slut!" he yelled again, thrusting his head up toward the ceiling. "I'll do whatever I want, you understand me?"

"Believe me, you won't."

Malcolm turned just time to feel Xander's fist ram square into his nose.

Mike ran around them and scooped up the boy, taking off for the door, regardless of the blood still leaking slowly from his arms.

Malcolm hit the floor hard, slamming his head on the coffee table. What remained of Charles' Frosted Flakes spilled onto the floor from the impact.

Malcolm passed out there, wedged between the couch and the coffee table, blood leaking from his nose.

One punch.

Squinting angrily, Xander leaned over and grabbed him, wailing his fist once more into the unconscious man's head just for good measure, then backing up twice and running to join Mike outside and bring the boy to the hospital.

Malcolm did not get up again until the police dragged him away, telling him to watch his head the officer put him into the back of the car. He turned, wanting very much to bite the officer.

Don't do that, Malcolm.

"Shut up, bitch."

CHAPTER FOURTEEN:
IN THE FUTURE

Mike took a deep breath as he followed Xander through the large, gray doors that led to Adam Genblade's bedside cell. Entering the room, the first thing he noticed was the smell: the peculiar odor that always accompanied unnaturally sterile rooms. It was somewhere between the smell of bleach and sugar water.

The walls, floor, and ceiling were all glimmering white, not an item out of place. It was like an exhibit at a museum, the ones that always looked too neat. Nobody lived like that, not in real life.

It took him a moment to notice the figure laying in a bed against one wall. The sheets were just as white as the room, devoid of stains or any sign of human life whatsoever. The man lying on the bed was barely visible through the mass of pipes and wires and needles poking out of him. His face was almost completely covered by a clear blue mask that allowed him to breathe through the thick plastic tubes shoved down his throat. The only movement in the room was the man's chest, rising and falling with a machine's calculated rhythm.

If it had been anyone else but Adam Genblade, Mike would have felt a great swell of pity for the man. In this case, it was only the slightest touch of pity that slanted his heart, making it so cold that he had to shiver.

"You sure you want to do this?" he asked, reaching out and touching Xander's shoulder. "You don't have to, you know."

Xander turned his head just enough to see his friend in his peripheral vision, then back to Genblade again. "Yes, I do."

He reached into his pocket and pulled out the Spider-Gem, held it up to his eye, and examined its gleam one last time.

"What is that thing, anyway?" Mike murmured, motioning toward the ruby.

"A hunk of glass," Xander responded in a condescending tone.

Mike shot him a look. "You know what I mean."

"And you know what I said. I really think it's nothing but a hunk of glass now."

"What made it so special, anyway? Why did LeGaea want it so bad?"

Xander frowned, taking another look at Genblade and then stepping toward the room adjacent to it, followed closely by Mike. "The three gems, when they touched or whatever... I saw glimpses, thoughts, feelings..." He turned to Mike, his eyes filled with a unique pain that his friend had yet to see on him. "I think it was my future."

Mike's eyebrows shot up. "What was it like?"

Tom Petty blaring on a loud speaker. Too loud. Burning

air. Pop tarts. Red. Blood red. Red. Red hair. Hurt. Pain. Hurt pain. Scream: too loud! Shattered. To ground. Look up. Smell of cream. Touch. Hair. Cheek. Grinding teeth. Death. Death! DEATH!

"I don't remember," Xander said dismissively, starting down the long row of lockers leading to the one that contained Genblade's belongings. "But it showed me where the boy was and what was going to happen to him if we didn't get there."

"That's kinda freaky," Mike said, motioning to the gem in Xander's hand again. "In that case, are you sure that we should be giving it up,?"

Xander tossed the stone into the air, catching it in his palm again. "Naw. The way LeGaea freaked, I think that you need all three for the mojo to work. Even if he hadn't run off, you smashed one of them pretty good. Like I said, this is just a hunk of glass now."

Mike sighed, letting his eyes get caught up in the gleam of the ruby for a moment. "Still, heck of a thing to just give up."

Xander shook his head. "I think it's overrated. I think that's been the point of all this... it's true what they say, man. Ignorance is bliss. There's no way that knowing too much about who we are or where we're going can lead to anything good."

Reluctantly, he nodded. "What was up with that LeGaea guy anyway?"

"Don't know. He wasn't after us, I think. There's been no sign of him since, and he left a pretty clear path of destruction wherever he went. Still, if he could see the future, you'd think he would have avoided us." He shrugged, opening Genblade's locker and taking out the Spider-Sword. Its sheen was magnificent, even after all those months of being locked away without use. The light reflected off it like a shimmering star burning brightly against the dull, colourless atmosphere of the locker room.

"Maybe the future's written. Maybe he couldn't avoid it."

"Run!" Mike yelled, as he forced Cathy ahead of him. The creature landed on all fours on the sidewalk. His glossy eyes studied their movements, how they ran. He found their weak spot at the sides. They'd both been damaged there. It moved like a jaguar, leaping to the sidewalk and then onto two legs to pursue them.

"Keep... going..." Mike encouraged Cathy, holding his side. They were almost to her house. But they'd both danced this dance before. He wasn't about to make the same mistakes twice. He cut through an old alley, hoping to run across the backyards of the complex until reaching her back door.

They could see the house now.

"Mike..." Cathy pleaded, grasping at her side. "It hurts."

"Now that's a scary thought," Xander mumbled, mostly to himself. He brought the gem up to its rightful spot on the sword's handle, and it clicked into place. The sword looked like a complete work of art now, restored to its natural significance.

"Still don't see why you had to do that," Mike ventured, gazing at the blade in fascination.

Xander frowned, putting it back inside the locker and closing the door. "Genblade killed the first woman I ever loved... but I killed his, you can't forget that. Taking this from him, it'd be like someone taking my last picture of Sara from me... it'd be wrong. Not even Genblade deserves to suffer like that. Nobody does." He started walking back toward the exit, and Mike followed. "Plus, Genblade's helped us out a lot since. In a weird way, I feel like I owe him."

They opened the doors, and both of them walked past the living corpse of Adam Genblade without so much as glancing at it.

"I don't feel that way anymore," Xander continued. "And if he ever wakes up from that coma, there won't be anything holding me back. It'll be just the two of us."

"I guess so," Mike nodded, stepping up to walk side-by-side with Xander. "Yeah."

"Besides, I had to try and get something positive out of this whole mess."

Mike gave him a quizzical look. "What do you mean? Me and Cathy are back on track, we defeated LeGaea, we saved that kid, returned the gem, and now that Malcolm creep is going to spend eternity times two rotting in Coral Beach Pen. And I didn't kill you. All in all, I don't consider that a bad day's work."

"I dunno," Xander breathed, glancing at the ground. "I feel like I lost this one. I wanted so much to be normal. To be like everyone else and have a girlfriend, and for the only thing on my mind to be a stupid school dance... but I guess I can't have that. Never will. I mean, fuck, why me?"

Mike took a moment to absorb that, then reached back and slapped his friend in that back of the head.

"Ow!" Xander cried out, though not really hurt. "What

the hell was that for?"

"For being an idiot," Mike said simply as the two continued to walk out of the police building. "You know what I think every time you say 'Why me'?"

Xander frowned, then shrugged.

"I think: why not you? Seriously, why not? For all your whining and bitching... and for all the times I've kicked you to the curb, you're doing all right. I can't think of one single person who would do better at what we're doing here. Someone's got to do it, so it might as well be you. And we'll figure it out eventually. I know we will. Me, you and Cat. And while we're figuring it out, we'll save some kids. Hell, I can think of worse ways to spend the day."

Xander smirked. "I guess so."

"Yeah," Mike laughed, patting his friend on the back. "We good?"

"Yeah." Xander responded, forcing a smile. "Yeah, we're good."

〤〤

Cathy walked up to the Walker house and took a long, deep breath. She knocked on the front door and Macy Walker answered, her eyes soaked with tears.

"What do you want?" Macy asked, without resentment.

Cathy smiled, her hand on her purse. "Can I come in, Mrs. Walker? There's something we need to talk about."

Three days later, a name was added to the Coral Beach Memorial Wall:

Kerri Walker - Kennessy.

Xander sat at the bar, took a puff of his smoke and flicked the ash into a nearby tray. His black shirt conformed perfectly to his body, making it look as though it had been tailored for him. He took another long drag, then extinguished the cigarette.

Just as he did, a woman walked in and sat next to him, taking off her coat and shaking off the late fall cold before motioning to the bartender to get her a drink. He nodded before moving to a different part of the bar to prepare the drink.

She wore a navy-blue blazer with white pin-stripes, matching slacks, and an off-white scarf around her neck that made her look professional. Her dark red hair was perfectly groomed, and her pale white skin was offset by blazing red lips. She looked powerful, in control of everything and every man in the room... except, of course, for the one she happened to be sitting next to.

"Megan Greene. What are the odds of finding you here?" Xander asked without looking at her, a wry smile spread across his lips. He motioned for the bartender to bring him a beer when he was done mixing Megan's drink.

Megan turned to him suddenly, as if not even realizing he was there before, but her look of shock quickly melted into a warm smile. "Xander. Long time, no see. How'd you know I was going to be here?"

Xander smirked. "You mean besides the fact that you come here every Saturday, order two absolute vodkas but only drink one and a half, then drive around downtown for a half hour to kill time before a date with Tony?" He glanced at her for the first time since the conversation began. "Just luck, I guess."

Megan slowly raised an eyebrow at him, even as the bartender handed her the drink. "Do I have a stalker now?"

Xander chuckled. "No. When you spend enough time in this town... you get to know things."

"I'll keep that in mind."

He looked her up and down, taking notice of her more expensive attire and the shape of a slimming body. "You seem to be doing well for yourself."

"Yeah. I'm high profile now thanks to you and your friend Adam Genblade," she smiled, taking a sip of her drink and fiddling with the olive in it.

"I wouldn't call him a friend."

"It was meant to be humorous," she said bluntly. "So, what brings you by here? Come to warn me of impending doom?"

"No," he laughed, accepting his beer and paying for it, then lighting up another smoke. "Just needed to see a friendly face is all. How are things?"

Megan rolled her eyes. "Terrific. I got rights groups breathing down my neck one way, and angry mothers the next over the Genblade thing."

"How's that?"

"Well, you remember those people who wanted him executed? The ones who didn't want their tax dollars going toward feeding a murdering sociopath?"

"Yeah?"

"Imagine how they feel now that their tax dollars are

helping keep him breathing."

"Ah," he mused, taking a long puff, then blowing it out. "Not too pleased, I take it."

"They're demanding they pull the plug. Bunch of savages, I tell you," she turned toward him, getting more involved in the unexpected conversation. "What about you? I see you've been keeping busy."

He shot her a confused look.

"That Malcolm guy. I heard about that. Good work, by the way. Top notch stuff."

"Could've gone better."

"You couldn't have caught him sooner, Xander."

"No," he scoffed. "The guy went down with one punch. I would have greatly preferred to have been able to wail on him for at least a few minutes."

"The nerve of some people," she drawled, rolling her eyes.

"Really. Do you think they'll have any trouble putting him away?"

Megan almost laughed. "Not likely. They found his mother's corpse propped up on the upstairs toilet, been there for at least a month. Guy said she was still talking to him, yelling at him."

"Yikes."

"Can you imagine someone being so loony as to talk to dead people?"

Xander paused, coughed once, then took a sip of his beer.

Megan observed the silence for a moment, then chose to disregard the topic. "So, what about you? How's life outside murder and mayhem treating you?"

Xander snorted. "I only just now found out I can't have one."

"Who says?" Megan nearly yelled, waving a hand at him dismissively. "I thought that way once, before Tony came along. You gotta make these things work, they won't just fall into your lap, y'know. What's the problem, anyway?"

Xander smirked. "It's a girl."

Her eyes widened, and she nodded smoothly, taking a knowing sip of her drink. "Gotcha."

"No, it's not like that..."

"What's it like then?"

"It's special. It's... something I never felt before, not even with Sara. It's a weird sense of belonging, like everything falls into place when I'm around her."

Megan nodded, encouraging him to continue.

"When she's around, everything else falls away. It's like: Julie! There could be a million other things going through my head, but when she's in the room, it's: Julie! And it's not like I'm ignoring everything else... no, when she's around, everything seems to work out for the best anyway. It's magic. She makes even my life simple, and every simple moment I have with her is just a gift... each one completely new and different from the one before."

"That sounds great," Megan smiled.

"Yeah..." he said, trailing off, wishing he could cry. "It was."

"Was? Why can't it be now?"

"Because," he hissed, taking back the rest of his beer. "I can't love her. Even if I could, I'd only hurt her."

Megan laughed. "Oh, sweetie."

"What?"

She leaned closer, adopting a motherly tone. "You know all that stuff you described?"

"Yeah?"

"That's love, babe. And even if it isn't, all those things are the best way to get to love. Believe me, I know. And as for that 'if you love her you'll hurt her' stuff... baby, that's par for course with any love. And that's not your choice to make. You need to let her decide if the risk is worth taking. Stop worrying about her and just... look inside your heart."

A light flashed in Xander's eyes, and he turned to her. He leaned in, kissed her on the cheek, then extinguished what remained of his cigarette. "I gotta go. Thank you so much."

"Anytime. Next time you gotta tell me how a kid your age gets in here anyway."

He turned and smirked at her as he headed out the door. "I keep telling you... I have my ways."

She watched him leave, laughing gently to herself as she motioned for the bartender to bring her a second drink.

꒳

Julie walked out to the front door and opened it, wanting only for the non-stop banging to end. She swung it open, a hard glare ready on her face for whoever was there.

"Xander," she said simply, watching him as he doubled over and tried to catch his breath.

"Julie!" he gasped, his lungs aching for oxygen.

"What are you doing here?"

"I had to tell you, I figured it out!" he blurted, taking another deep breath. "I know what it means now, I got it. Well, Megan got it, but I'm here now and you're here and that's all that really matters, right?"

She looked at him, and a smile spread across her lips as she held onto the door.

He smiled back, the first honest smile he'd worn in days.

"Xander," she started, her voice calm and even.

"Yes?"

"I've got a hell of a lot of thinking to do about us," she said bluntly, then slammed the door in his face.

EPILOGUE

It's like a dance. Mandy wrote in her journal as Xander walked alone down the front steps and out onto the sidewalk. He was holding back the tears he had wished for days ago, and was now sorry he had. *Nobody really knows the beat or the moves... or really even what song we're all grooving to, but we all keep dancing anyway, because we can't bear to sit one moment out... even if sometimes we end up looking stupid, like, doing the Macarena or something. But in the end, that's all life is: a dance.*

Mike and Cathy are back together, and by the looks of Mike, that's for the best. He's so happy now, happier than I've seen him in a long time, and me and him really get along now. Me and Cathy, too, as weird as it sounds to, like, write that down, or even say. I'm just glad he's okay. I wasn't sure for a minute there.

Cathy got over the whole pregnancy thing. Well, probably not over it, I'm sure, but she's doing a lot better, and that's always good. She put a name to her pain, and that's always the way to do it. I guess you can't just let things like that linger around, or when you turn your back on it, it'll kill you.

Julie's been crying a lot. I don't think her and Xander did it... but I think maybe it was something worse. Like, maybe something worse than sex can happen with a boy. I know that... falling in love is probably the worst pain ever. There's no end to it, but we still crave it more.

Like black licorice.

She didn't come out of her room all weekend after Xander left, not even to tell me to turn my music down, even though I only had it turned up that loud so she would finally come out. No matter how loud the music got, though, I could still hear her crying.

Xander hasn't been talking a lot. He's back to his same old routine, letting life pass him by again, keeping to the shadows, skulking a lot. He's still super nice to everyone, even me, but it's different now. Tommy says he's seen him like it before, right after some girl named Sara died. Said he's gone back to that place again, the dark place where everyone has to go at some point in their lives, but where Xander seems to live. Hopefully he'll get out of it again soon, I liked him better when he was all right.

And me... nothing really changed with me. I guess if someone else was writing this, they'd tell you that I sat this dance out, that I didn't do anything. That I was standing still. But really, I danced with everyone. They just didn't realize it. They all think I'm a loser, that I'm not even important.

᚛ᚷᚔᚐᚁ᚜

Dr. Warren O'Toole sat on his chair in his office, one leg crossed over the other. He scribbled handwriting only he could understand on his notepad, which was placed uncomfortably on his lap. With his free hand, he waved his pocket watch back and forth in front of Mandy's unconscious face, holding her in her deep, hypnotic trance. "What did you say, Mandy?"

"The Black Angel came... the Black Womb... he came and saved everyone... he always does... he looks so awful, but he's really sweet and kind... he's my friend... Mike's my friend..."

"You still believe Mike Harris to be the Black Womb, Mandy?" O'Toole asked, scribbling away.

"Oh, yes... I saw him... he saved me... he's so nice..."

O'Toole flicked back through his notes, then continued writing, stopping once to adjust his glasses. "Does the Black Womb have strange eyes or fingers?"

"Yes... his eyes are red, and his fingers have claws...not all the time, though, not when he's Mike... and the claws can go away, he touched me and didn't even hurt me... saved me..."

"Does it look anything like the creature that attacked the school earlier this month?"

"No... yes... it looks different... strange... it was different..." the girl's brow furrowed.

"Tell me more about him, Mandy." O'Toole pressed. He put down the pad and leaned forward, smiling.

They all think I'm a loser, that I'm not even important.

Boy, are they in for a surprise.

PREVIEW

BECOMING

PREVIEW
BECOMING

Julie Peterson walked through the halls of Coral Beach High School, well aware of the fact that she was being watched. Stared at. Some even gawked, but mostly just those who rode the little bus to school and simply didn't know better, in her opinion.

She didn't mind either way.

She was more than used to being looked at, talked about, and secretly sworn upon. It had been happening to her for her entire life, and today was no exception. Except for the fact that today, they all would be given a good reason to stare.

Her shirt was loose on her and not at all appropriate for the weather outside. It was a bright purple and came down across her arms in long, open sleeves. The neck was ruffled and bunched so much that it looked like she had a scarf on with it, although the material was so airy it wouldn't have provided any insulation. It was actually much more conservative than her usual attire, and she'd almost put it back and not worn it several times. In the end, the choice had come down to one simple fact:

It was one of his favorites.

The rest of her ensemble, her makeup, even her jewelry had been chosen on similar merits, right down to the choice not to conceal the freckles that dotted her cheeks. He'd always said he thought they were cute.

She stormed down the halls, her eyes filled with a grim determination and a spite that had become her trademark. Coming into the lobby, she took a long look around at who was there, standing about in the pre-class melee. After just a moment, she spotted her prey.

Xander Drew sat in one corner, his eyes far off and distant. Mike Harris, Cathy Kennessy, Tommy Irons and her cousin, Mandy Peterson all stood near him, talking about something stupid no doubt. He seemed oblivious to the rest of them.

She walked right up to them.

Cathy noticed her first, her eyes growing wide.

Julie walked right up and tapped Xander twice on the shoulder.

Slowly, Xander turned around to face his girlfriend, knowing it was her before he even saw her just by the smell of her perfume and that feeling he got in the pit of his stomach when she was close by. He smiled at her. She had sparkling green eyes and freckles that ran across her cheeks and the bridge of her nose no matter how much lemon juice she applied to them. Her hair was never the same way twice, always highlighted a different way so that she was always fresh, always new. Always beautiful.

"Hi," he said simply, when he realized that he was staring at her.

She smiled, then leaned in and opened her mouth. She kissed him in front of everyone, her tongue going in and out of their view as it darted between his mouth and her own, her hands traveling a mile a minute as they danced everywhere over him, squeezing him closer, grabbing at his muscular arms and abdomen. Her lips were soft, so soft, and yet the way she used them was so hard and powerful that it made his head swim, hard to think.

She broke off the kiss and stepped back, leaving he and every other person around awestruck. She smiled at him, tilting her head to one side and letting her hair fall over her shoulder in a way he'd always found adorable.

"Xander..." she said softly, soothingly. "... It's over."

With that she spun on her heels and started to walk away toward the front doors.

"Julie!" Xander called, shaking off the effects of her kiss and taking off after her. He almost tripped once, still light headed.

Cathy's face cringed as she watched the event, wanting to close her eyes and yet completely unable to, like the way people stopped to watch car wrecks even though they didn't want to see what had happened. Even though you'd have nightmares for a week, you just couldn't miss it. Mike squeezed her hand tight, frowning. She did the same.

Mandy shook her head and sighed, looking as though her eyes might soon well up with tears.

Tommy just stood there, dumbfounded. After a moment, he elbowed Mike. "Did you see that kiss?"

Mike rolled his eyes.

"Julie, wait!" Xander called again, catching up to her

as she neared the exit and taking her by the arm.

"Get your fucking hands off me!" she screamed loudly, whirling around and drawing the attention of anyone who wasn't already watching.

Warren O'Toole stopped talking to Principal Shnieder, turning around and cocking an eyebrow at the scene.

Xander obeyed, letting her go immediately. "I'm sorry, I just... what was that Julie?"

"That was a break up." she said matter-of-factly. "A damn good one, if you're me. Just ask any girl here outside of Cathy and Mandy, and I'm sure they'll agree."

"Can't we talk about this?" Xander whispered between clenched teeth, very aware of the crowd.

"I've done all the talking I was going to do, Xander, but if you wanna talk... fine! Let's talk!" she yelled, shoving him back a pace. "Let's talk about the way you started off by rejecting me time and time again, making me feel like crap! Huh? Or, would you rather talk about all the ways I tried to be everything you wanted, and every time I did, you changed what you wanted! Or maybe..." she snarled, pointing toward Cathy. "Maybe we can talk about your little crush on her, hmm? Come on... everybody else is!"

The crowds gaze shifted momentarily from Julie to Cathy, who tried her best not to lock eyes with any one of them. Mike smiled at her, and suddenly she didn't care what they thought.

"Julie, please." Xander pleaded, his eyes filled with hurt. "Julie, don't do this. I thought you said you - "

"Yeah? Well I don't. Guess you're not the only one here who can change his mind, huh?"

She snarled at him, then turned to walk away. This

time he made no effort to stop her, just watching her hips swing from side to side in a triumph, even if that triumph was over him.

She reached out to open the door, when suddenly it swung open hard and fast, catching her in the nose! Blood started to spew forth from it as she fell back, hitting the tiled floor like a ton of bricks, scraping her hand as she did so.

The door cracked against the wall, shattering the plaster there and sending small chips to the floor.

Ian Char and Duncan Combs stepped into the school, their big, black hiking boots making long streaks on the floor. Ian looked down at the bleeding Julie and smacked his lips at her, giving her a quick double kiss before reaching into the front of his pants and pulling out a gun. Duncan followed suit, pulling two similar handguns from behind him, aiming at nobody in particular but causing screams of fear from everyone nonetheless. On each of their right arms was a bright red letter T tattoo, their sleeves ripped off to accent it, hiding it from no one anymore.

"What the hell?" Mike swallowed, taking a long step forward. Cathy pulled him back. Taking note of the guns, he nodded.

Xander clenched his fists. The Womb organ swelled up inside him, the beast banging at the doors, ready to explode from his veins and take them down.

He suppressed it.

There were too many people around that would see, and Julie might get hurt if there was a firefight. He took a step forward, leaning down to pull on Julie's shoulder.

From between Ian and Duncan, Randy Owchar

stepped into the school, brandishing a shotgun and his very own Tee tattoo.

Xander quickly got Julie to her feet and back into the crowd, where Tommy's teeth could be heard clenching above the screaming and yelling. Randy had killed Tommy's best friend, Sud, in order to gain entry into the Tees. Right in this very hall, he'd shot him in cold blood.

Randy noticed Xander and aimed his gun directly at him.

"Hold it!" he bellowed, although his voice didn't really suit his attitude. Not deep enough. Not that anyone was going to argue the point with him while he was brandishing a sawed-off shotgun.

Xander froze immediately, raising his hands in the air. He might... might be able to survive a blast at this range, depending on where it hit, but there was no guarantee that nobody else would get hit either.

"Turn around." Randy ordered.

Again, Xander complied, biting his lip about the fact that he knew he could take down that son of a bitch child-killer in ten seconds flat.

"Well, well, well," Randy smiled, shaking his head at Xander. He lowered his voice considerably, so that only he and Xander could hear. "If it isn't the Black Womb."

Slowly, Xander's eyes went wide, as he started to realize what that feeling he'd had was all about...

FROM THE AUTHOR

I've got to say, in looking back over the Coral Beach Casefiles books many years after they were written, I'm shocked at how well they hold up. I don't mean to toot my own horn with that... you have to understand, I'm a writer who is very critical of my own work, especially my early work. I tend to look back and only see the warts. So in the years since the character of Xander Drew has moved on to his own eponymous series, I tend to look back on this one as 'that one where a kid goes missing and then for some reason there's a treasure hunter that has very little to do with the plot.'

I think I forgot until re-reading it (and re-reading the edits that were but in by Eryn Heidel and Erin Vance -- thanks much to you both) why those things were there and why they were the way they are. Because this isn't a book about a weird treasure hunter or even about a missing child (that was the last book). This is a story about Xander and Julie, and the rest is just... fluff. And I don't say that to be dismissive, if you like those elements! But in re-reading it I remembered why they were there: to demonstrate the worst and the weirdest parts of the world that Xander is withdrawing from into the arms of Julie Peterson. They're there to illustrate the two types of threats he comes up against: off the wall scifi-fantasy threats and horrible all-too-human threats. And he's running from both right now, into some small pocket of normalcy.

If you read this book, I really hope you enjoyed it. I was really finding myself as an author during these. I wrote this particular one during college. These books were borderline experimental at times... but man, I still dig that dialog. I maintain that you can get away with a lot of crazy shit as an author so long as your dialog is good. I enjoyed this looking back more than I thought I would, and I sincerely hope you did, too. The next book, Becoming, brings the storyarc to a close in a big finish: you're going to want to be there for it.

This book, like all my modern work, is dedicated to my partner in all things, Ellen Curtis. To my amazement, she read these books and stuck around anyway.

Matthew LeDrew

July 15, 2019

ENGEN TIMELINE

With over twenty novels spread over three different series by many different authors, the Engen Universe of titles is growing every day and into genres we couldn't have imagined! From the original ten book *Coral Beach Casefiles* thriller series, its crime novel sequel series *Xander Drew*, our flagship adventure title *Infinity*, or single-novels like *Jacobi Street* or *light|dark*, there's something in the Engen Universe for everyone with more books by more authors on the way soon!

...But how do the events relate to one another, chronologically? While some astute readers have guessed at the potential timeline (some accurately, some not), we're going to finally set the question of the Engen Timeline to rest.

Turn the page for an up-to-date guide of the ever-widening world of Engen, featuring the works of Ellen Curtis, Andrea Hackett, Sarah Thompson, Jay Paulin, and Matthew LeDrew!

In the 10 Years Prior Black September

"Reptilia" by Matthew LeDrew
published in *light | dark*.
Danger descends on a small secluded town in the form of a deadly virus with fantastic and terrible side-effects. Can a small group of doctors escape alive?

Compendium by Ellen Curtis
Three short stories forming the basis for the Engen Universe's ties to suspense, genetic engeneering, and the supernatural. Features the stories "The Tourniquet Revival," "Falling into Fire" and "At Midnight, the Dawn."

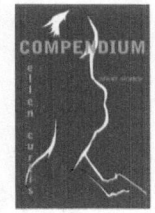

"The Theogony" by Matthew LeDrew
published in *light | dark*.
A tale of young Theo Flaherty of the *Infinity* series and his time admitted against his will to the Black Springs hospital, where he learns to paint, and seeks out his father.

Black September

"Revving Engen" by Matthew LeDrew
published in *light | dark*.
A direct lead-in to both *Infinity* and *Black Womb*, Tasha travels to Coral Beach, Maine on a hot tip about a recently discovered young man with incredible abilities.

Infinity by Ellen Curtis & Matthew LeDrew
Faced with a destiny he's uncertain of, the enigmatic Victor must bring together four unique people with very special abilities… or face the tasks ahead alone. Guaranteed to excite!

Black Womb by Matthew LeDrew
Fifteen years ago, something happened in Coral Beach, Maine that resulted in the present death of a seventeen-year-old boy. Now four high-school students must try to solve the mystery… before the killer picks them off.

Jacobi Street by Matthew LeDrew
When a mysterious painting shows up at an art gallery he works at, Bob must work with Eddie and Sloan to track down its sinister origins and convince the people living on Jacobi Street of them, before its too late!

Transformations in Pain by Matthew LeDrew
When two girls are assaulted and one is hospitalized, the residents of Coral Beach must put their shared tragedies behind them and stop the man responsible, as well as unlock the secrets behind the true nature of the Womb…

Year One: October

Smoke and Mirrors by Matthew LeDrew
The approaching trial of Genblade brings closure to the people of Coral Beach, until people start showing up dead in the same manner they did when he was at large.

"Scarlett" by Andrea Hackett
published in *light | dark*.
Introducing Scarlett, the slightly damaged hunter on a mission to save others from the monsters from her past.

"The Inevitable" by Ali House
published in *The Lightbulb Forest*
A young woman must contend with the
emergence of a frightening new power alongside
the emotional high of a first date.

The Tourniquet Reprisal by Curtis & LeDrew
A man lives in Atlanta, Georgia that people
don't talk about, but everyone knows he's there.
He arrived a year ago and turned a gaggle
of uneducated youth into something new,
something to fear.

Roulette by Matthew LeDrew
As the teen suicide rate in Coral Beach starts to
climb astronomically fast, Xander travels to Los
Angeles to fight his most terrifying adversary
yet... and learns that the only thing worse than
looking for release... is finding it.

Year One: November

Exodus of Angels by Curtis & LeDrew
Victor's enigmatic past is illuminated when
Jaycee accompanies him to visit a new friend
in the paliative care ward of the Black Springs
hospital, where Theo also happens to be
searching for a cure for Leigh.

Ghosts of the Past by Matthew LeDrew
Coral Beach faces its most awesome threat when
one of Engen's past mistakes is unleashed upon
the unsuspecting populous. Friends and enemies
unite to fight a common enemy... but will even
that be enough?

Touch Your Nose by Matthew LeDrew
Simon Monk must infiltrate the San Fransico
branch of Shane Industries, a massive company
with deep ties to the Engen Universe. Where do
his true loyalties lie? And can he get out without
causing harm?

Ignorance is Bliss by Matthew LeDrew
After being set through the ringer one too many
times, Xander decides that his life with Julie
needs a little more attention… which is bad news
because a new villain has come to town with his
sights set on Adam Genblade.

"Gristle While You Work" by Jay Paulin
published in *light | dark*.
A short story centering around the rise of a new,
and possibly cannibalistic, serial killer in the
Engen Universe.

Becoming by Matthew LeDrew
For months Xander Drew has been doing his
level best to keep the streets of Coral Beach clean,
which means it's time for the forces of darkness to
strike back… all at once.

Inner Child by Matthew LeDrew
Julie is hospitalized with life-threatening wounds
to both body and soul. But the real threat comes
from the hospital walls themselves, as a demonic
presence makes itself known to Xander and his
friends.

End of Year One

Gang War by Matthew LeDrew
The Tees, a homicidal gang of evil men, has finally been taken down by Xander Drew. But his victory is short lived, as retired Tees are mysteriously killed. With a town of suspects, anyone can be the culprit... including one of their own.

Chains by Matthew LeDrew
Sociopath Derek Smith has been freed from prison and is praying on the weak; and none are weaker than August Styles: a pregnant girl with Down Syndrome who has run away from home.

"Omega" by Ellen Curtis
published in *light | dark*.
A sinister division of Engen begins a series of experiments on pregnant women in a fashion eerily similar to those that created the original Black Womb project.

The Long Road by Matthew LeDrew
Xander meets the American people — and realizes that the world is harsh and wicked, but can also be soft and gentle, even loving. Xander Drew comes of age on the road, and sets his new direction.

Year Two

Cinders by Matthew LeDrew
Detective Horton enters a violent and dangerous world he didn't know existed beneath the veneer of order and structure that he has based his entire deductive method around.

Sinister Intent by Matthew LeDrew
One of the killers Detective Horton could not
catch has resurfaced: a serial killer who flaunts his
sinister intent in front of the Los Angeles Police
Department, making it so that no one is safe.

Faith by Matthew LeDrew
Xander's mysterious and troublesome past returns to
haunt him on the streets of Los Angeles; a place where
even more people can get caught in the crossfire of the
games of death and deceit that makes up his life.

Flickers in the Night by Matthew LeDrew
Lisa Rowdan is hunted by her haunting -- and
powerful -- ex-boyfriend Ryan through a lonely
city street. Can she escape him?
One of over twenty great sprine-tingling short
stories!

Family Values by Matthew LeDrew
Xander and his new friends Crowley, Lisa, and
Tim investigate a series of kidnappings and
murders that stretch back decades, all of which
have the same similar twist: victims being found
after years of being missing.

The Future

Fate's Shadow by Matthew LeDrew
When one of Xander's old cases comes up for
trial, Megan Greene returns with it. The former
friends are led into conflict regarding her client's
innocence. However, they put their difference
aside when they both become targets of the
vigilante known as Shiro Gilbert.

The Future

"Remers" by Sarah Thompson
published in *light | dark*.
In the not-too-distant future of the Engen
Universe, young athletes are the targets of a
scouting program to create the next stage of super
soldier with cybernetic enhancements.

The early years of **Xander Drew** as he struggles with the evils of his small rural hometown of Coral Beach, Maine. Cursed with the heart of the Womb and the gift of seeing the world around him for what it really is, Xander must learn the hard lessons about the nature of humanity to traverse the minefield of criminals, gangs, and abusers that stand between him and ultimate happiness -- but most of all that **sometimes it takes a monster, to catch a monster.**

"THE WRITING OF ITS GENERATION- - VISUAL, TO-THE-POINT AND IN-THE-MOMENT."
- The Northeast Avalon Times

The Coral Beach Casefiles series by Matthew LeDrew:

For more information, please visit

www.engenbooks.com

THE XANDER DREW SERIES

Prologue: The Long Road (December 2019)

COMING SOON FROM ENGEN BOOKS:

FATE'S SHADOW

A violent past case is reopened as Xander must contend with Detective Thomas Horton, the vigilante Shadow Flame, and a returning figure from his youth in Coral Beach -- all while trying to prevent a murderer from running free. Can Xander stay the course even as his world crashes in around him?

ABOUT THE AUTHOR

Matthew LeDrew holds an Honours Degree in English from the Memorial University of Newfoundland with a minor in Anthropology, and studied Journalism at College of the North Atlantic in Stephenville, Newfoundland. He was honoured to be a jury member of the 2018 NLBA awards.

He has written twenty novels for Engen Books: the ten book *Coral Beach Casefiles* series, *The Long Road, Cinders, Sinister Intent, Faith, Family Values, Jacobi Street, Touch Your Nose, Infinity, The Tourniquet Reprisal, and Exodus of Angels* the latter three of which with co-author Ellen Curtis.

He lives in St. Johns, Newfoundland.

www.ingramcontent.com/pod-product-compliance
Lightning Source LLC
Chambersburg PA
CBHW022153240626
47153CB00007B/2635